The Girls in the Velvet Frame

The Girls in the Velvet Frame

Adèle Geras

HAMISH HAMILTON:LONDON

© 1978 Adèle Geras
First published in Great Britain by
Hamish Hamilton Children's Books Limited
90 Great Russell Street
London WC1B 3PT

ISBN 0 241 10011 9

Photoset, printed and bound
in Great Britain by
REDWOOD BURN LIMITED
Trowbridge & Esher

For Beryl

Note: The 'Ch' in 'Chava' is pronounced as in Johann Sebastian Bac*h*

There is no intentional resemblance between the people in this story, and what happens to them, and actual people and events.

PART ONE

Chapter I

SUMMER, 1913

THE HEAT lay thick and yellow over the house, and around three sides of the flagged courtyard the shutters were closed against the sun. Shrivelled geraniums drooped among brown leaves in the earthenware bowls on the balconies, and the soil was cracked and red, a miniature desert around the cacti, standing in a cluster of pots in one corner of the yard. A small cat, belonging to no-one in particular, sand-coloured, with limp, white paws, slept stretched out in a square of shade, his thin sides trembling with each breath. On one doorstep, watermelon pips sprinkled with salt were drying in the sun on a round, brass tray. Washing, on lines strung across from one balcony to another, was baked stiff, and hung motionless in the still afternoon.

The house, built of square, yellow stones, stood at the bottom of a winding, cobbled street. Six families lived in it. Sarah Bernstein and her five daughters had three rooms and a kitchen on the upper floor, on the cooler side of the house, the side that was in the shade during the afternoon. Their shutters were open to catch any stray breath of air, and the whole family was gathered in the only room that was not strictly a bedroom. The girls called it a dining-room, and certainly that was where all the meals were eaten. But it was, too, a parlour for receiving guests, a study for quiet reading and writing, a sewing room, a music room, a playroom: a room for living in. It was also Sarah Bernstein's bedroom. At night, the em-broidered coverlet and cushions vanished, sheets and pillows were brought out of the linen chest, and the sofa was transformed into a bed.

On this afternoon in August, the dining-room was all dressed up for company. The heavy furniture had been polished, a red velour table-cloth with long fringes lay over the table, and even the best jug, of rose-patterned china, was covered by a little muslin veil weighed down with coloured beads, to keep the flies out of the milk. The girls were fidgeting. Rifka and Chava, the two eldest, sat on high-backed chairs at the table, itching in their high-necked, long-sleeved dresses. Naomi lay against the cushions on the sofa, wishing that she could take her shoes and socks off, and put her feet down on the cool tiles; and the little ones, Dvora and Shoshanna, perched on two stools beside the door, pouted and asked for drinks, and made patterns on the dusty floor of the balcony with the toes of their shoes.

Then Mrs. Gluckmann arrived, wheezing and panting up the wooden stairs, shimmering in her violet dress and black straw hat, brow damp, chins wobbling, and padded bosom heaving. Sarah Bernstein poured the tea at once, and over the biscuits and the cakes, Mrs. Gluckmann recovered a little. She said:

"And what do you hear from Isaac, Sarah? What a lovely boy! How you must miss him, all of you. How is America?"

Sarah Bernstein paused. The girls said nothing. Their elder brother, like the young son in all the fairytales, had left Jerusalem nearly a year ago to seek his fortune in America. There had been no word from him. For months they had been waiting and hoping and nothing came. Anyone who asked for news was told what a long journey it was—the Atlantic was such an ocean, well-known for its width, the ships from Europe infrequent and well-known for their slowness, and so on, and so on. But today, Sarah Bernstein smiled and said:

"Yes, we had a letter. A wonderful letter. Isaac has found a good

4

job, in a jeweller's shop, and lives with a nice Jewish family. He has his own room, he earns a good wage, and thank God he is healthy. What more can you ask? Why don't you have another cake, Zehava?"

The three elder girls were silent, dumb with amazement. Their mother was lying! Naomi opened her mouth to protest, but Rifka frowned and kicked her sharply on the shin under cover of the table-cloth. Chava looked quickly at the little ones, in case they should say something, but they were busy feeding their rag-dolls on the sofa, and had heard nothing. Mrs. Gluckmann was delighted. She said:

"Show me the letter, Sarah. You know Isaac was always a favourite of mine."

Mrs. Gluckmann, a widow, owned a prosperous bakery. Rifka was soon to start work there, and she knew that Mrs. Gluckmann wanted her youngest daughter to marry Isaac. She had often spoken of making him a partner in the business, but Isaac had no desire to be the owner of a bakery, not even of a very good and prosperous one. She also knew (although she never said so, except to her sisters) that Ruth Gluckmann was enough to make anyone take fright and run away to America. But now she leaned forward anxiously. What would Mother say next? The letter—how could she not show it off to her friend? Sarah Bernstein said:

"Such a pity! I have lent it to my cousin. Another time, perhaps. But enough of my children. How are your daughters?"

Mrs. Gluckmann smiled and reached for her handbag.

"I have a surprise for you. A present, because I know how fond you are of them. Perhaps I will also send one to Isaac if you will give me his address. I know that he and Ruthie were good friends."

Before her mother could speak (would she have to give a false address?) Chava broke in:

"What is it, Aunt Zehava? Do show us."

Mrs. Gluckmann fumbled in her bag.

"It's a photograph of my girls. There, for you. I had a dozen copies printed."

She put the photograph on the table, and everyone crowded around her to have a look.

"It's beautiful."

"Marvellous!"

"It's exactly them, exactly them."

"How artistic! How tasteful!"

"Shoshie want to see. Let Shoshie see!"

"And me! And me!"

"When did you have it taken?"

"What pretty dresses!"

"Ooh, how lovely!"

All the voices rose together in a great chorus of excitement. Rifka whispered to Chava while the others were still exclaiming:

"They look quite ordinary, really. Just as they always do. But it's so clear. You can see every stitch of the lace. And the patterns on the vase the plant is in. It's like magic." Then the stories began.

Mrs. Gluckmann told of the studio, the photographer, the box on legs called a camera, the way the girls had to pose, and the black cloth cover over the photographer's head when he took the picture. Every detail was revealed. She paused for a moment at the end of the saga, to catch her breath, and to refresh herself with more tea.

"Just half a glass, Sarah, my dear. My throat is quite dry from telling you everything. Oh, it was a great excitement. My girls are still talking of it. You know", she added, stretching her hand towards the cake-plate, "in America they must have photographer's studios on every street. You should write to Isaac and tell him to have a portrait taken, and he should send it to us all. Yes, that's a very good idea. Maybe I'll write to him myself."

6

"No, no, Zehava dear, I'll do it. The very next time I write," said Sarah hurriedly, pushing glasses and saucers across the table in some confusion.

It's not surprising that she's anxious, thought Chava, after all those stories she's just told. She was just about to change the subject, when Mrs. Gluckmann swallowed the last few crumbs on her plate, and began to speak again.

"Talking about Isaac, you know, makes me remember the old days, Sarah, when your dear husband was still alive, blessed be his memory. Isaac as a little boy, aah! Never, never have I seen such eyelashes. A sin, I used to say, to waste such eyelashes on a boy. Do you remember how I used to say that?"

"Yes Zehava, I remember very well, and he was a lovely baby."

"He was spoilt," said Chava firmly. Sarah, Mrs. Gluckmann, Rifka and Naomi turned shocked faces to her.

"How can you say that?" said Naomi. "He was so kind and lovely. He used to play with me, and tell me wonderful stories and teach me songs. How can you say he was spoilt?"

"It wasn't his fault," said Chava calmly. "We all loved him, and did everything for him, and fetched and carried for him all his life. Can you remember saying 'No' to him ever, Mother?"

"Well, of course I must have done, as I've done to all of you. Especially when he was tiny. I can't recall any particular time, but I must have done."

Chava was silent, remembering very clearly one day when she was five, and Isaac was twelve. She had been given a horse of carved and painted wood. It had red wheels, and a long red, wool tail. All morning she had played happily with it, shrinking in her imagination until she was small enough to ride on its back, through the pine forests under the dining-room table. And when Isaac came home from school and saw it, he decided he must draw it at once, that very minute. Chava could still hear, now,

7

that conversation from so long ago:

"I want it just to draw," he had said, smiling. "Please, darling Chavale, I'll give it back later."

"No."

"But you can have one of my soldiers."

"Don't want your soldiers. I'm playing with my horse."

"Mother, make Chava give me her horse for a while."

Sarah had said: "What do you need it for? It's her horse, a toy for babies."

"I want to draw a picture of it. Please Mother, tell Chava to lend it to me. I promise I'll give it back."

"Come Chava," Mother had said, "give it to him and he'll make a picture of it, and then he'll give it back. Here, you can come and help me shell the peas."

And I gave him the horse, thought Chava, without a fuss. I must have known, even at that age, that it was useless to cry, that that was the rule: Isaac had what he wanted.

Mrs. Gluckmann was in the middle of an anecdote showing how charming Isaac was.

" . . . and when he came into the shop with your bread order (he couldn't have been more than seven!) he used to say: 'Is it true you give a *bagel* to boys who are specially good?' Well, imagine the cleverness? Who could resist him?"

"And when I was ill," said Sarah, "after giving birth to Shoshie, and he was fifteen, hours he sat with me, reading me books, and telling me all the marvellous things he would do when he was a man." Sarah wiped a tear from the corner of her eye.

It was easy for him, thought Chava. It's always easy for boys and men. Meanwhile, Rifka was cooking, cleaning, feeding the baby, walking with Shoshie in her arms half the night so as not to disturb the neighbours, and I was keeping Naomi and Dvora out of mischief, and quiet, so as not to disturb Father, and His Highness was reading stories from the depths of an armchair!

"And he took me to school the first day I had to go," said Naomi, "and he came right into the class and spoke to the teacher, and said: 'Please take special care of my little sister', and the teacher said he would, and he did, and it was all thanks to Isaac. And he met me every day for weeks and weeks and brought me home."

"That's Isaac all over," said Mrs. Gluckmann, "kindness itself."

Everyone nodded in agreement, Chava noticed, sighing a little to think of him so far away.

"It was natural, I suppose, for him to want to leave," said Sarah. "So many opportunities for him there, that's what he said, and he said he would come back and visit us when he's rich, but who knows, who knows? Sometimes I feel I'll never see him again, never." Sarah rose from the table, and went towards the kitchen. "I must slice more lemon for the tea," she said at the door. "I'll come back in a moment."

Mrs. Gluckmann leaned across the table towards Rifka. "She's very sad, I can see, my dear. Are you all helping her and keeping her cheerful?"

"Yes, Aunt Zehava, we're trying," said Rifka quietly, "only it's quite sad for us as well. We miss him too, you know."

"Yes, my dear, of course I know that. I'm sure you're all doing everything you can. You must all be a great comfort to poor Sarah, I can see that."

"Here's the lemon," said Sarah, coming into the room. "Now, have another glass of tea, Zehava, and tell me where you found that lovely hat."

"This old thing? You don't mean to tell me you've never seen it before? Well, just one more glass, and then I must go. It's getting very late."

At last the sun went down, and down the steps creaked Mrs. Gluckmann on her way home. Sarah Bernstein waved to her friend from the balcony, and then went into the dining-room where the girls were nibbling at the last few biscuits, and piling up cups and saucers, ready to take them into the kitchen. She smiled.

"Well, there! Wasn't that fun? Lucky Zehava! But luckier me. What a picture *you* would make, my little girls, my bunch of roses."

"Mother," said Rifka, "you're talking like that because you don't want to talk about the other thing."

"What other thing, Rifkale? What are you talking about?"

"Isaac, Mother, Isaac. Why did you tell all those lies? You've told us never to do it. Now what are we supposed to think?"

Sarah sat down on the nearest chair, and began to pick at the fringe of the table-cloth.

"I know. I'm sorry. Perhaps I was wrong. I don't know. I started to speak, and then it was too late to stop. It's because I don't want to be pitied. Zehava telling the whole town: 'Poor Sarah! Her son left her, and doesn't even bother to write. He's no good.' I don't want them to talk like that about your brother. God will understand, I mean it for the best. And besides," she looked up defiantly, "it could be true, couldn't it? It could all be exactly as I've said, only he hasn't told us yet, that's all. It could be the truth." She laughed. "Don't look so serious, girls. Truth! No one can tell the truth all the time. Worse than lying is hurting people. Should I tell Zehava she looks like an armchair? Or that her daughters are not as pretty as mine? Of course not, so I say she looks well, and her daughters are lovely, and everyone is happy. Do you understand?"

"Yes, Mother," said Rifka, a little doubtfully.

"And you, Chava? And Naomi?"

"Yes, Mother, I suppose so," said Chava.

"If you say so, Mother," said Naomi.

"Good, then help me clear the table, Rifka, and you, Chava and Naomi, can start to put the little ones to bed."

Rifka and her mother left the room carrying dishes. Naomi went out on to the balcony to find Dvora and Shoshanna, and Chava was left alone, standing beside the table. She picked up the photograph and looked at it carefully for a few moments. The name and address of the photographer was printed on the back. Chava propped the picture against the fruit-bowl on the sideboard. Then she stood with one arm delicately resting on the back of the chair, and her head tilted to one side, and that was how Naomi found her.

"Come on, Chava. They're ready now. Whatever are you doing?"

"Posing like Ruth Gluckmann. Pretending to have my photograph taken," said Chava. "What's wrong with that?"

"Nothing, only Dvora's hair needs plaiting."

Chava sighed. "It's silly to pretend, really, I'd love to be photographed, but you heard how much it costs."

"Well, pretending is free. Maybe one day, it'll happen."

"Maybe tomorrow it'll snow! Come on, Naomi, let's go and do the hair. They must be nearly asleep."

"I'm coming," said Naomi, and she followed her sister along the balcony to the bedroom where Dvora and Shoshie were waiting.

"I suppose now," said Rifka, "we'll all have to tell the same story, if anyone asks us."

"Then we'd better make sure we know all the details," Chava said. "You especially, Naomi. You know how absent-minded you are."

"I'm not," Naomi whispered. "It's just that I'm usually thinking about something else."

"Yes, well don't," said Chava. "You'll have to think about this and remember every word Mother says, and stick to it, if anyone asks you."

Rifka, Chava and Naomi were kneeling on Rifka's bed, and looking out of the window at the street below. The yellow light of oil-lamps shone from the windows opposite, and made soft, black patches of shadow on the walls, and in the corners of buildings. The sun had gone, but the heat still hung over the city, and what little breeze reached the girls in their long, white nightgowns was like the rush of air from an oven, just opened.

"I wonder," said Rifka, "if she's right. I mean, wouldn't it be strange if all those things were true? That's how it would be in a story."

Naomi said: "I've imagined Isaac riding in carriages, and dining in cafés, and working in a bank."

Chava snorted. "You two! You're as bad as Mother. It's all nonsense. It's not true, none of it. We don't know where he is, or what he's doing, and that's that. He could be dead, for all we know."

Naomi turned pale. "Dead? Oh, Chava, don't say it! Say you don't mean it."

"Why should I? You and your stories. Well, I can make up stories, too. He was swept overboard in a gale, he caught a dreadful disease on that terrible, crowded ship, no one would give him work in New York, and he had nowhere to live, and starved to death—making up stories is easy."

"Don't! Stop! I don't want to hear." Naomi was weeping now, wiping her nose and eyes with the hem of her nightgown. "I can't bear it if he's dead. Say it's not true. Please, say it isn't true, Chava."

"Oh, heavens, now look what you've done, Chava. You're always doing it. You know she misses him, and you know she believes everything. Go on, tell her it's not true."

Chava sighed. "Eight years old, and nothing but a crybaby. You *know* it's not true. I'm sorry I made you cry, but you are stupid. He's probably perfectly all right, but too lazy to write. He *was* lazy, you know."

"I know," Naomi sniffed, "but I wish he would write, otherwise it seems as if your stories are truer than mine and Mother's. When I go to America, I'll find out, but it's such a long time."

Rifka laughed. "Oh, so you're going too, are you? When, exactly?"

"When I'm sixteen," said Naomi. "Only eight more years, and then I'll go. I'm saving the money. When I get to America, I'll ask and find him."

Chava giggled. "She'll ask! Listen to her. Who will you ask?"

Naomi thought for a while, then said: "People, I expect."

Rifka and Chava bounced back on to the bed, and rolled around, helpless with laughter.

"What are you two laughing about? What's so funny?" Naomi sounded cross.

"Oh dear," said Rifka. "'People', you said. Have you any idea how many people there are in America? In New York, even?"

"The same as here," said Naomi.

"There are millions," said Chava. "Do you know what that means? Millions, and millions and millions, like sand on a beach, or stars in the sky. Millions more than here. You'd never find him."

"Oh, Chava, you've done it again," said Rifka. "She's crying! Come on, Naomi, don't be silly. Stop crying, and get into bed. If you get to America, then I'm sure you'll find him. You could go to the Rabbi, or something. Don't worry, you'll find him. Anyway, he may write and give us his address before you're sixteen. So go to sleep now, and stop snivelling."

The girls left the window, and lay down on their beds. No one said anything for a long time. Then Naomi started snoring softly.

"Chava," Rifka whispered, "are you awake?"

"Yes."

"I wish you wouldn't make Naomi cry just before bed. It makes her snore, and then I can't sleep."

"Think of pleasant things, that's what Mother always says."

"What's pleasant?"

"Winter's coming, that's pleasant. You're prettier than Ruth Gluckmann, that's very pleasant. And tomorrow we're going to visit Mimi, that's very, very pleasant. Is that enough? I can't think of anything else. Rifka?"

Rifka was silent. Chava kicked her top sheet into a crumpled heap at the bottom of the bed, turned over and closed her eyes. Soon she, too, was asleep.

Chapter II

This, thought Naomi, is the best part of the day, the cool time, the early morning. Early rhymes with pearly. Pearly morning. Out on the balcony she leaned against the wooden railing and watched the sky bleached of colour slowly turning pale yellowy pink, like the skin of an unripe peach. The sunlight, light without heat, fell through the door that stood open onto the street, and sloped into Menahem Friedman's rabbit hutch on the other side of the court-yard. The rabbits were awake. Naomi could see pink noses pressed against the wire netting, and one black ear poking out of the top. The Friedmans called the rabbits Black and White—just like that, which showed, thought Naomi, what dull people they were. There were so many other pairs of names: Jacob and Esau, Cain and Abel, David and Jonathan, and that was without even think-ing carefully. Dvora and Shoshie loved the rabbits, and called them Blacky and Whitey. They spent many hours trying to feed them with leftovers from the vegetable basket. Menahem, skinny little wretch, teased them and pinched their arms and tried to frighten them away, but the girls always went back the next day to try and stroke the ears and noses, and feel the little twitching mouths nibbling the leaves from their hands.

Soon, the noises would begin. Dvora and Shoshie would fall out of bed and run along the balcony in bare feet, and down the stairs and across the courtyard in their nightgowns, if they weren't stopped, trying to reach the rabbits before Menahem got up.

15

Mother would rise next, wash herself in the basin of water in the kitchen, dress, and prepare the morning meal, lighting the wood in the small oven, to warm the bread, which was fresh, and scattered with poppy seeds. Then she would lay the table, putting out milk and cheese and a dish full of honey. If the little ones come out now, thought Naomi, I shall stop them. If they listen to me. They listen to Rifka, she's the eldest, almost their mother, and anyway, everyone listens to Rifka. Everyone obeys her. And Chava, well, she's only eleven, it's true, but she's clever, and knows the right thing to do, and people seem to do what she wants without noticing. I'm in the middle, not one of the big ones, so no one obeys me. But if Dvora and Shoshie come out now, I'll at least get them to dress before they go down, and then they won't be doing what Mother calls 'parading their nightgowns in front of the whole world.' I'll go on with the princesses story. They like that.

The old house was waking up. Mr. Friedman came out on to his balcony, dressed only in his trousers and vest, and began to splash noisily in a basin of water set on a chair. He had hairy arms. All that black hair curling along his arms like fur, thought Naomi, in this heat. It must be like wearing a knitted jacket. Mr. Friedman had a fish-shop near the market, and sometimes brought home bundles of skin and fish bones for the sand-coloured cat. From the room directly below where Naomi was standing came the drone and mumble, like faraway bees, of the Old Man's morning prayers. If anyone knew his real name, they never used it. He lived alone, a tiny, black-coated figure with a wrinkled white face, shuffling between the house and the synagogue in soft shoes and a moth-eaten fur-rimmed hat. Sometimes he would sit in the shady part of the courtyard, reading heavy books with thick, yellow pages, and mumbling, always mumbling to himself. He must be very holy, Chava said once, because only God's ears are sharp enough to catch what he says.

"Naomi! Naomi!" The little ones were awake. They had tip-toed up to their sister so silently that she jumped at the sound of their voices.

"Ssh! You'll wake everyone."

"Mother's up already," said Dvora. "Rifka and Chava are snoring. Can we go feeding the rabbits now?"

"Go and feed the rabbits, you mean. Yes, soon, but you must wash and dress first."

"No, rabbits first." Shoshie's face began to crumple ready for tears.

"Dressing first," said Naomi, trying to sound firm, like Chava. "And if you're good, and don't cry, I'll tell you some more about the princesses."

"Will you?" Dvora began to bounce up and down. "Will you tell us a lot?"

"Yes, come along and wash your faces and hands, and then I'll tell you lots and lots." Naomi gave a hand to each of the little girls, and pulled them into the kitchen, where she began to scrub their faces with a cloth.

"Did I tell you, for instance" (as Shoshie tried to wriggle herself away from the wetness that was going to come down and cover her eyes) "that the princesses had rabbits?"

"Really? Real rabbits?" Dvora stood quite still as the wet cloth came towards her.

"Oh yes, amazing rabbits. On the same lawn where the peacocks lived, d'you remember?"

"With the fountains."

"That's right. There was a lawn in front of the palace with fountains and peacocks and marble statues."

"And rabbits," said Shoshie. "Coloury rabbits."

"Of course, all the colours you can think of: black and white and brown, and pink and orange and mauve and even green

17

rabbits."

"Aren't any green rabbits," Dvora said smugly. Naomi often thought her little sister had no imagination, but she only said:

"This is a magic land. Rabbits are all colours. Any colour you want. And spotted. And striped. And flowered."

"What did they eat? Did they eat vegetables?"

"No, vegetables were too ordinary. Come and put your clothes on."

In the bedroom, Naomi found Dvora's dress, neatly folded on her chair. Her shoes stood side by side next to the bed, which looked as if it had hardly been slept in at all. Naomi sighed. Dvora was too tidy. It didn't seem right in a child of five.

"You can dress yourself, Dvora, and I'll do Shoshie."

Shoshie's clothes lay all over the floor, and Naomi gathered them together, ready to pull on to her squirming little sister. Dvora began to brush her hair, standing on tiptoe to see into the square mirror hanging on the wall.

"So what," she said, "did they eat, if vegetables were too ordinary?"

"Who?" said Naomi.

"The rabbits in the princesses' garden."

"Oh, them." Naomi frowned, and tried to think herself back into the story. "Well, they had lovely things, like strawberries."

"And cinammon cake," said Dvora.

"Yes, and potato pancakes."

"Grapes," said Shoshie.

"Certainly grapes. Now stand still, Shoshie, and let me brush your hair."

Dvora had folded her nightgown, and placed her pillow over it and smoothed it down, and now she sat waiting for Shoshie.

"What happened to the rabbits?"

"Nothing," said Naomi. "Why should anything happen? They

18

just lived happily in the garden."

"That's boring. Make something happen. An exciting thing."

"A monster got into the garden. Please stop twisting your head round, Shoshie. How can I do your hair?"

"What monster?" Dvora wanted to know.

"No monster. Please, no monster," wailed Shoshie.

"Alright, no monster. Maybe a dragon that eats rabbits."

"Not eat rabbits! Don't want! Don't want!" Shoshie's voice was rising to a shriek.

"Be still, Shoshie. I'll make the dragon go away. There, he's gone. The rabbits are quite safe. Now come and have breakfast."

As they left the room, Shoshie ran ahead. Dvora took Naomi's hand and said mournfully:

"I wanted a monster. I wanted something to happen. Shoshie never lets things happen in the story. Boring. She's just a baby."

"Well, perhaps we'll have a monster, and not tell her."

"Yes. Good." Dvora was pleased. Her own private monster. "Was he terrible?"

"Yes, terrible. Ate twenty rabbits a night for supper. But the Golden Prince—d'you remember him?"

"Yes, he was the princesses' brother."

"That's right. Well, he's going to fight the monster soon."

"Really? Is he going to kill the monster?"

"Wait and see," said Naomi. "I'm too hungry to do any more now. Next time, I'll tell you about the fight."

"But not in front of Shoshie."

"No, for her we'll keep it nice and peaceful."

When Naomi and Dvora came into the dining-room, the other girls were already sitting round the table, eating. Rifka was cutting a slice of bread spread with honey into squares.

"There, Shoshie," she said, setting the plate down. "Lots of little

19

honey bricks. Eat each piece, and when they've all gone, you'll see the flowers on the plate.''

"Basket."

"That's right, they're in a basket. Now eat it all up."

Shoshie began to pick up pieces of bread. She poked her tongue out to lick off a little honey, then put the bread down again.

"Don't want."

"Eat, Shoshanna," said Sarah, "or you will not go with your sisters to visit your aunt this morning."

"Oh, Mother, why do you speak of her like that?" Chava bit into a crust and chewed it angrily. "'Your aunt' in that cold, horrible voice! Our father's sister, she is. You shouldn't be so unfriendly. He loved her, and we love her. You hate her!"

"Silence, Chava! I do not hate your aunt Miriam, it's not true. And I always let you go and visit her."

"Miriam. She calls herself Mimi," muttered Chava.

"Silly Frenchified nonsense! Miriam is her name, and Miriam I shall call her."

"What has she ever done to you, Mother?" put in Rifka, more mildly.

"Done? Nothing. Why do you think she's done something?"

"It's always as if you disapprove of her," Rifka explained. "You never go to see her, or ask after her or anything."

Sarah frowned. "Well, I *do* disapprove, I suppose. I don't see why I have to deny it. I've told her so to her face, many times."

"But Mother," said Naomi, "what is there to disapprove of? She's the kindest, gentlest, sweetest, prettiest person in the world." She stopped suddenly, uncomfortably aware that a mother was supposed to be all those things.

"Her clothes," said Sarah. "All those mauves and pinks, like a sweet pea plant, and the scent! Heliotrope up your nose till you can hardly breathe, and feathers and jewellery—she's got no business at her age, looking like that."

"Why not?" asked Dvora.

"Because . . . (and you're too young to be joining in this conversation, Dvora. Eat your food and kindly don't interrupt again.) Because, I said, women of our age should be. . . ." Sarah looked all round the room, feeling for the words ". . . dignified and mature. Yes, that exactly: dignified and mature." Pleased with these two words, she sat down and stirred her glass of tea.

"But she's so interesting, Mother," said Rifka. "Really. She tells such lovely stories."

"I know. I've heard them. Operas in Vienna, and casinos in Monte Carlo and cafés in Paris. I've heard them all. Stories! She should try bringing up six children on my money, then she'd have stories, and what stories!"

"Once," said Naomi, "she let me put on all her necklaces, every single one. Fat pearls, and rubies, and glittery diamonds."

"Diamonds, you say." Sarah laughed. "Would she live in two poky little rooms above the butcher's if they were diamonds? False is what they are. Glass, that's all."

"I don't see that it matters what they are, as long as they look pretty," said Naomi.

"That just shows how little you know," said Chava. "Grown-ups only think things are pretty because they're worth a lot of money, not the other way about."

"I don't understand what you mean, but you don't have to be so horrible to me." Naomi's voice trembled.

"Leave her alone, Chava," said Rifka. "No-one wants her going to Mimi's with red eyes."

"Do rabbits like bread-crusts?" asked Dvora. "We're going feeding the rabbits now."

"Rabbits like bread-crusts," said Sarah, "but from this family they won't be getting any. Eat them up, Dvora, and then I'll give

21

you some carrot-tops and cabbage leaves I've left specially."

Dvora could be seen weighing up the bargain: rabbits against bread-crusts. The rabbits won. She pulled a face, and began to eat.

"A blessing, the rabbits are," said Chava. "Those two would never do anything we told them if Menahem had no rabbits."

"Now can we go, Mother?" Dvora's plate was clean, and so was Shoshie's.

"Yes, go now. The vegetables are in a bowl on the kitchen table. Take the bowl too, but remember to bring it back. I've got enough to do today without running to Friedman's in search of forgotten bowls."

The little girls ran out of the room, and could be heard squeaking with pleasure as they clattered down the stairs and across the courtyard.

"Now, Rifka," said Sarah, pouring herself some more tea, "there's something we have to discuss. You remember I told you about the Levinsky's, don't you?"

Chava giggled. "Oh yes, the family of Rifka's betrothed, the love of her life!"

Rifka frowned. "Don't be silly. I've never even met him, so how can he be the love of my life?"

"I hope he is the love of your life for your sake, if you're going to marry him."

"I don't have to marry him if I don't like him, do I, Mother?"

"No, no Rifka, of course not. But I would like you to meet him, and try to be nice. Don't close your mouth and blush as you sometimes do in company."

"I don't."

"You do," said Chava and Naomi together.

"They are," continued Sarah, "such a nice family. Mrs. Levinsky is a real lady. And the house, wait till you see it, Rifka."

"When are we going?" said Rifka, looking down at her hands.

"On Thursday, to take tea in the afternoon. I'll press your pink muslin."

"Thank you." Rifka was thinking of being a bride, not playing any more, not being able to be a child. But that's stupid, she thought, I haven't felt like a child for ages, not since Shoshie was born, and Father died and Mother was sick. I looked after everyone then. But a bride. With my own house. Not to sleep in the same room with Chava and Naomi any more. I wonder if I'll like him? What do you say to boys? Isaac is the only boy I've known properly, and brothers surely don't count. But I don't have to marry him. Not if he's ugly, or unkind or boring. I don't have to, but it would be good if I did. Mother would be pleased. The family must be quite rich. Maybe he's handsome and good, and I'll have a white dress, silk, and long to the ground, and my hair up, and a veil, and the canopy from the synagogue like an embroidered sky, clear blue, and spotted all over with golden stars.

Chava and Naomi were silent as they cleared the table. Poor Rifka, Chava was thinking as she put the breakfast dishes into the sink, but she's the eldest, I suppose, and has to do the expected thing. But she never finds the expected thing difficult to do. I can see her whole life: husband, children, housework, everything. Boring, boring, boring. If they make me marry someone, I shall run away. I'm going to be famous. Maybe a famous explorer. Strange lands where no-one has ever been before, that's what I'd like: deserts, jungles, plains of ice as far as you can see. I'm not spending every morning of my life doing dishes, like this. Oh no.

Naomi was quiet too as she dried the plates. There was a red-striped towel for meat dishes, a blue-striped one for milk dishes, and the girls were never allowed to mix them up. Milk and meat dishes were two separate things, and it was God's ancient rule, Naomi supposed, that meant you could never have milk in your tea when you'd just been eating beef stew, or a cake with cream, or

23

even bread and butter. Those things were kept for milk meals. Mimi (and this was one of the forbidden, exciting things about going to see her) does not keep a Kosher house, as Mother never ceases to point out. We eat the proper things when we go there. She makes an effort for us, for our father's sake, but she tells us stories of meat actually cooked in a cream sauce, imagine! But, of course, that was in Paris. Rifka will probably be very strict in her own house, when she's married. She thinks that kind of thing is important. Chava won't even think about such matters. I'd like to ignore it, too, but what if it's important to God? Maybe he would punish me if I ate cream cakes and meat in the same meal? But Mimi's alright. Perhaps God has more important things to worry about, but you never know, and it would be taking a risk.

"Naomi, for heaven's sake, look where you're putting those plates. They'll crash to the floor in a minute."

"Sorry. I was thinking."

"About Rifka? Yes, so was I. Poor old Rifka! Would you like to spend the next three years sewing household linen till your eyes are dropping out of your head, and then be married when you're sixteen? I can hardly think of anything worse."

"I shall be going to stay with Isaac in America when I'm sixteen."

"I forgot, of course you are. But you can also get married in America, you know."

"But it'll be different there. Modern, I'm sure. And I'll buy my sheets and pillowcases in a shop."

"If you have enough money."

"Oh, Chava, why do you do it? Squash people's dreams absolutely flat till there's nothing left of them? I *will* have money, and I *will* buy my things in a shop, so there." Naomi flung down the tea-towel, and ran out of the room. Chava sighed. Naomi's dreams! Perhaps it was unkind to squash them, as she put it, but didn't she

24

know that only sadness and disappointment came of dreams? Still, perhaps I'd better say something nice to her or she'll be in a sulk the whole day, and spoil going to Mimi's. Chava wiped her hands on her apron, and went to find her sister.

Dvora and Shoshie were crouched over a bowl of dead geraniums, drawing patterns in the dry earth, with sticks. The carrot-tops and cabbage leaves were now bulging out of their apron pockets, and the bowl lay empty on the paving stones. They were waiting, as they did every day, for Menahem Friedman to have his breakfast and leave the rabbit hutch unguarded for a few minutes. Menahem, a skinny little boy of six, had elbows which were knobbly and hard, and left bruises when he pushed the little girls with them. His nose was pointed, and his eyes were set so far apart in his head that he looked a little like an animal himself. He knew that Dvora and Shoshie would run to the hutch and begin to feed the rabbits the minute he left the balcony, but there was nothing he could do to stop them, for when his mother said breakfast she meant it, and woe betide the poor child who did not come running when called. He had, however, perfected a method of eating his meal in five minutes, and then out he would come again, on to the balcony, ready to push the girls away from the hutch.

This morning Mrs. Friedman was taking longer than ever to prepare the meal.

"Cabbage," said Shoshie. "Shoshie want."

"No, Shoshie," said Dvora, "you've got the carrots."

"Want cabbage."

Dvora sighed. "Baby! Here, have the cabbage and I'll do the carrots. Give them to me."

"No, Shoshie want carrots."

"But I've given you the cabbage," wailed Dvora, fully understanding in that moment, the exasperation of her mother and elder sisters when it came to dealing with Shoshie. She wasn't fair, she wasn't reasonable. How did they manage to get her to do what they wanted? Dvora only knew one way.

"Give me some food now, this minute, or I'll pull your hair. Hard."

Grudgingly, Shoshie produced a little rabbit food and handed it to Dvora.

"Good," said Dvora. "Now let's pretend to play till it's safe. I'll tell you when we can go."

They watched Menahem when they thought that he was not looking. He was cleaning the hutch, putting in new straw, and filling the rabbits' bowls with water. Then:

"Breakfast, Menahem. Come at once," boomed Mrs. Friedman, and strode on to the balcony with her sleeves rolled up showing her fat, pink arms, and carrying a jug of milk in one hand. With the other she grasped Menahem by the shoulder, and turned him towards the door. As he disappeared out of the sunlight into the darkened room beyond, he turned round and stuck his tongue out at the girls.

"Now!" said Dvora, and taking Shoshie's hand, she ran across to the Friedman's balcony.

As they pushed cabbage leaves through the holes in the wire and into the quivering pink mouths, Dvora thought: they're happy to see us. I expect they like us better than that stupid boy. He doesn't stroke them like we do. Shoshie was fondling Blacky's ears through the top of the hutch.

"Hurry, Shoshie, give them the food. He'll be out in a minute."

Shoshie began pushing pieces of food through the netting so quickly that Blacky and Whitey became confused, and then frightened, and finally huddled together at the back of the hutch, so as not to be engulfed by the sudden avalanche of titbits.

"Gone. Dvora, rabbits gone!" Shoshie looked amazed.

"And we must go. Come on, he'll be out soon. Do you want him to kick you?"

"Want Whitey," said Shoshie. Dvora began to pull her towards the courtyard with one hand, but Shoshie stood firmly near the hutch with her feet apart, and stuck all four fingers of her other hand through the holes in the wire-netting. She began to wriggle them about, hoping the rabbits would come and investigate. Whitey had just begun to edge carefully towards them when Menahem rushed out of the dining-room, flapping his arms and shrieking:

"Get away, horrible creatures. Leave my rabbits alone. They're my rabbits. Not yours. You have to ask my permission." He began to approach Dvora with his fists raised.

"Put your fists down, you bully," said Dvora in a trembly voice. "You're frightening my little sister. Aren't you ashamed?"

"No. Go away. You're not supposed to touch the rabbits without my permission."

"But whenever we ask you, you always say no," shouted Dvora.

"That's because I don't want you to touch them. They're mine."

"Well, if you never let us touch them properly, with permission, we have to do it when you're not there, and then you catch us, and get angry, and hit us. If you let us stroke them sometimes, when you're there by the hutch, then we wouldn't come and try to do it when you're away." Dvora smiled, trying to be friendly, but Menahem was not so easily diverted from the morning drama which he had come to expect.

"Well, I don't give you my permission, and now I'm coming to kick you."

The girls scrambled into the courtyard. Menahem ran after them, but they were too quick for him today. The stairs up to the Bernstein's rooms were, by tacit agreement, safe territory, and

27

Menahem had to stand furiously outside the Old Man's door, while Dvora and Shoshie pulled faces at him from a safe distance.

"We fed the rabbits, we fed the rabbits, we fed the rabbits," they sang at him, and he turned round, stuck his hands (still clenched into fists) into the pockets of his jacket, and made his way back to his side of the house, kicking with his heavy brown shoes at sticks and little bits of gravel. The girls watched him going, and giggled together. Then Dvora spotted the bowl, lying near the geraniums, and sighed.

"We've left the bowl behind again, and I'm not going to get it. I'm scared." She frowned, and then said happily: "But Naomi will get it for us. He'll never hit her—she's bigger than him."

Chapter III

"In one second, I shall have melted away in this heat, and all that you'll have left of your poor sister will be a pair of shoes and a hat," said Chava wearily, as they made their way to Mimi's flat.

"We're nearly there now," said Rifka soothingly, partly to Shoshie, whom she had been carrying on her hip for most of the walk, and partly to herself, to give herself the strength to put one foot in front of another on this day when all the buildings shimmered like mirages in a haze of heat, and everyone they passed moved slowly, like people in a dream. The sky could not be looked at: an endless expanse of pure white, burning light that hurt the eyes. The girls bent their heads and stared at the dusty ground and their own foreshortened shadows: small bodies, and the distorted outlines of their straw hats.

In Mimi's flat, the only light was the glow seeping through the slats of closed shutters, and the room was deliciously cool in the near-dark.

"Darlings, how brave you are to trudge through this heat to see me. But I'm so glad you did. First, sit down and have something cool." She poured a drink made of fresh lemon juice, sugar and water from a thick, stone bottle into five dainty glasses, and the girls drank, and looked around them with pleasure.

On the wall facing the window there were two pictures: one of a nymph wearing very few clothes leaning against a fountain, the other of an impossibly pretty lady engulfed in a tide of flowers painted in all sorts of unlikely colours. The chairs were covered in very old blue velvet, and the cushions were fat, satin ones, mauve and plum-red, embroidered with gold thread, and intricately patterned. Bowls of opalescent glass with wavy rims were filled with Turkish Delight from Mimi's unending supply, and lay around on small tables inlaid with mother-of-pearl patterns for guests to eat whenever they wanted to. It was sticky, full of nuts and cherries, powdery with sifted sugar, and felt like soft jelly when you squeezed it between your fingers.

"May we go and play in the bedroom, me and Shoshie?" Dvora asked when her glass was empty.

"And what will you play, my chicken?" Mimi smiled.

"We'll dress up as ladies," said Dvora, as she said every week.

"Very well, then, run along," said Mimi, and the little girls skipped out of the room.

In Mimi's bedroom, nothing was ever put away. Whispery chiffon scarves drifted over the back of the chair, silk shawls, like the wings of huge butterflies, and pink ostrich-feather boas hung out of the open drawers. The necklaces that Naomi loved so much were draped over a corner of the mirror in a waterfall of shining pieces of glass and pearls the size of peas. On top of the chest of drawers was a brush with a silver back, and a comb with a silver handle, a bowl of powder, a pink, swansdown puff, and rouge in little round pots made of bumpy glass, with silver lids. "From the good days," Mimi used to say, "when I knew the kind of gentlemen who bought me such things."

In the living-room, Rifka, Chava and Naomi told Mimi all about Mrs. Gluckmann's visit, and the photograph. She listened to their story and then: "You should have a photograph taken," she said, licking Turkish Delight sugar from her pink fingertips. "I've even got a pretty frame somewhere. I could find it, if I looked." She waved a hand at the decorative mess that surrounded her.

"Wouldn't Sarah be proud to have a picture of her little girls? On that grim black sideboard, perhaps?"

"Yes, but Mimi, the money," said Rifka. (Mimi was never "aunt". It was too ageing, she said.) "Where can we find the money?"

Mimi snorted. "Money! Humph! You don't want to let a thing like not having money stop you. Once the photograph is taken, there it is—the money will turn up from somewhere. God, as they say, will provide."

"But what if he doesn't?" said Chava. "He never provides much for us."

"That's no way to speak of God, my love. He provides for those who have the courage to go out and get what they want."

"But Mimi," said Rifka, "if we have our photograph taken without paying for it until later, we'll be in debt. That's a terrible thing, Mother says. It can ruin people, that's what she says." Chava and Naomi nodded. Mimi laughed:

"There's debt and debt, you know. I owe something to every stall in the market, and yet when I go shopping, the stallholders fall over their feet, bowing and scraping. And why? I'll tell you why. It's because I act rich. I put on clothes like a princess, I walk about as if I could afford to buy the entire market. I charm all the people with flattering words and pretty smiles, and they fill my basket, and never worry about payment. Every month, I give a little bit of money to each one, and that assures them that the rest is coming. And it does come. In time."

"It sounds easy for you, Mimi," said Naomi, "but we can't possibly act rich, like you. Our clothes would give us away. And Mother would kill us if she found out." Privately Naomi thought that owing money was rather wicked—all right for people like Mimi, who were daring and modern, but dangerous and sinful for ordinary mortals.

"Then I," said Mimi, "will have to arrange it for you. Next week when you come, we will go to the studio. I'll make an appointment, and I shall pay. Surely you won't mind owing me a little money. I will contribute half the amount, because I would love to have a picture of my little nieces and you, someday, sometime, will find the rest. I won't press you for it, I promise. Do you agree?"

Rifka, Chava and Naomi looked at one another. Naomi said:

"I have a little money saved up, but that was supposed to be for going to America."

"I didn't know," said Mimi, "that you were leaving. Aren't you a little young? I left home when I was seventeen."

"I'm going when I'm sixteen."

"Well, that gives you eight years in which to find the fare, but I think we'll let you keep your money, nonetheless."

"But what will we tell Mother?" asked Chava.

"Are you mad?" Mimi raised her eyebrows. "Don't breathe a word. She must never, never find out."

"Oh, Mimi, she's bound to find out. After all, we're going to give the photograph to her. In a pretty frame."

Mimi frowned and pouted. She twisted a strand of hair around her finger, then her face cleared and she smiled.

"It will be too late then to do anything about it. It will be what the French call a 'fait accompli'—something that's already been done. And besides, it will be so beautiful that even your mother will have to agree it's worth every penny. She might even be willing to pay the photographer something." (Mimi secretly considered that anyone who lived as quietly as Sarah probably had some money hidden away. Those who treasured their security, she thought, usually saw to it that they had some security to treasure.)

"No, if it is to be a present for Mother," said Chava, "then *we* must pay. Somehow, sometime. Otherwise it's not the same thing.

Let's do it, Rifka, please let's."

Rifka thought for a moment. Soon, she would be starting work in the Gluckmann bakery, at least until her wedding. She could put away a little of her wage, each week, and then there were birthdays, and *Hanvkah*, and oh, surely, surely for such a good cause, God would provide. She nodded.

"Yes. We'll do it."

Chava and Naomi jumped up and danced around the room with their arms around each other. Mimi clapped her hands. The little ones, who had been playing with scarves and shoes and pots of rouge in the bedroom, came in to see what all the excitement was about.

"Not a word to them," hissed Naomi, "they'll tell."

"Tell what?" asked Dvora.

"Nothing, little busy bee," said Chava.

"Was something! I want to know!"

Mimi gathered the little girls into her arms.

"I'll whisper," she said.

Rifka, Chava and Naomi stood quite still, as Mimi whispered to Dvora and Shoshie.

"How could she?" Naomi mumbled. "How could she betray us like that?"

Dvora and Shoshie wriggled happily among Mimi's lavender-coloured draperies and then squeaked:

"Oh, yes, watermelon! We want watermelon!"

"Watermelon?" said Naomi.

"Yes, I'm afraid I had to tell them our secret. Rifka and Naomi, you stay here with them, and Chava and I will trot down to the market for a moment and buy a watermelon to have after lunch. Come, Chava, follow me." Mimi rose to her feet, winked at the older girls, picked up a flower-strewn hat that lay on the table, and pulled it firmly down over her curls. Chava, wondering at her

33

aunt's ingenuity, ran out of the room behind her. When they reached the street, she said:

"Are we really going to buy a watermelon?"

Mimi laughed. "We'll have to, I suppose. We can't disappoint the babies. Luckily the market is quite close, or we should faint with the heat. But let us, as they say, kill two birds with one stone, and walk around the corner to see Monsieur Gustave, the photographer, and arrange everything for next week."

"You know him? The photographer? You know where the studio is?"

"Know him? Why, we grew up together. His name is Gustave like mine is Ophelia."

"Then why does he call himself Gustave?"

"Because it's French, and elegant, and artistic and inspires confidence. Shmuel, although there's nothing wrong with the name as such, does not."

"Is he nice? Does he like you?"

"Like me? He nearly died for love of me. Wrote me such poems, you could cry reading them. Sent flowers and chocolates, too."

"Then why didn't you marry him?"

Mimi considered the question. "I'll tell you my trouble, Chava, I'm too fussy. Always I thought the next young man would be that much better, richer, handsomer, kinder, more amusing. If I had my time over again, perhaps I should know better." Mimi sounded wistful. "Maybe it's not too late . . ." she sighed. "Well, it's too late for me ever to have lovely children like you. Did you know that I envied your mother?"

"I can't believe it!" Chava exclaimed. "What is there to envy? She moans about her hard life from morning till night, and although I'm sure it's not as bad as she says, it's true that she never finds time to sit down."

"But she has you, and your sisters, and even one day she may

34

have Isaac again. And in the course of time grandchildren, even great-grandchildren, if Rifka goes through with this marriage. When she grows old, she'll never be alone. To you, with your sisters around you, and at your age, probably to be alone sounds like heaven. Am I right?"

"Yes, I'm afraid it does."

"Ah, but at my age, it's the one thing in the whole world I fear. Being alone when I'm old."

"But you needn't, Mimi, you know that. We'll all love you and look after you as if you were our mother. You can live with me when you're old, and I'll take care of you, I promise." Chava looked closely at her pretty aunt, at the smooth powdered cheeks and the curling hair, and saw, with a sudden shock to the heart, the lines around her eyes, the wrinkled skin of her neck, and the blue veins standing out on the backs of her hands. She said, loyally: "Anyway, I can't imagine you ever being old."

"Well, I will be, though I try and push it a little further away by still doing pleasant things and wearing pretty clothes. Still, I expect I'll come as a shock to poor Max after all these years."

"Max? Who's Max?"

Mimi put her hand to her mouth in horror. "Oh my goodness, did I even forget to tell you about Max? It just shows how old I'm getting. But then you did start on the photograph without letting me get a word in, so perhaps it's not entirely my fault. Max, then. Well," Mimi took a deep breath, "I had a letter last Friday, out of the blue. Did I remember Maximilian von Eschenloer from Strasbourg? Could I recall the summer of 1885? The Comédie Française in Paris? A performance of Molière's 'Don Juan'? And the young soldier who spotted me through his opera glasses and came down in the interval to invite me to his box? Did I remember," Mimi waved a hand about vaguely "all kinds of romantic and passionate things from those days? Well, of course, I remembered at once. I had been called home to my father's funeral in the middle of this perfect romance, and hadn't heard from Max again, till this week. The letter came to your house, of course, which is where we lived when we were young until my brother married your mother. She must have told the postman to bring it here. Did she not even mention it to you?"

"I saw her talking to the postman the other day, but we're used to that. She often asks him if there's a letter from Isaac. I think she thinks he hides them at the bottom of his sack and loses them."

"Anyway, Max, it seems has always wanted to visit the Holy Land, as he calls it, before he dies (he's a Catholic, of course) and thinking of the Holy Land made him think of me. Would I be so good as to deign to see him again after an unforgiveable silence lasting so many years? He is widowed, he said, so it appears that he managed to console himself quite well after my departure. Still, it will be interesting to see him. You can't believe how handsome he was, how tall, how his eyes shone, and what a lovely, blond moustache he had . . ." Mimi sighed.

"What a marvellous, marvellous story!" said Chava. "Do you think you'll marry him? When is he coming?"

"Soon. Next month, although he doesn't say exactly when. Marry him? At my age? After having escaped fancy-free for so long? I doubt it."

"But Mimi," Chava was puzzled. "You said you wanted not to be alone, you wanted someone to look after you in your old age."

Mimi smiled. "I talk a lot of nonsense sometimes! Max is much older than me. He must be sixty by now, at least. What do I need an old man for, to worry over at my time of life, just when I should be relaxing and resting a little. Don't you know how tiresome old men can be?"

"But what if you'd married him then, long ago?"

"My father would have treated me as though I were dead for

36

marrying a Christian. There would have been mourning in the house, can you imagine such a thing? No, I've never understood it. I've always believed a man is what he is, and religion doesn't matter. But all the same, I'm glad I didn't marry him. Think of all the fun I should have missed, if I had." Mimi fell silent as they walked, and a look of sadness passed across her face. She said: "But children, now that I do regret. I would have loved to have children. Thank God for all of you, that's what I say." She smiled, and like a cloud passing over the sun, the sadness disappeared. "Come," she said, "let's buy that watermelon now."

"No, Mimi, we can't go and see Monsieur Gustave carrying a watermelon. Rich people never take watermelons with them wherever they go, I'm sure. We'll get it on the way home, and then we'll only have to carry it a short distance."

"That," said Mimi, "is what I admire about you, Chava. You are so practical and clever. Onwards chez Monsieur Gustave, then. Perhaps we'll see his skinny harpy of a wife. It'll make him regret his youth when he sees me, never fear."

The smells of over-ripe fruit and spicy meat and dust and sweat mingled with Mimi's scent, and her dainty white leather shoes picked their way through old melon rinds and cabbage leaves and torn scraps of paper. The crimson silk of the roses on her hat glittered in the sun, and as she walked, she waved and smiled at the stallholders, like a queen acknowledging her subjects, and they waved and smiled back. Chava walked beside her aunt, like a lady-in-waiting, as they left the market behind them, and made their way to the studio of Monsieur Gustave, round the corner and down the hill, in a more refined part of town.

"And then what happened?" Naomi wanted to know.

"Well," Chava paused. The girls were sitting on their beds, Rifka and Naomi eager to hear every detail of Chava's visit to the photographer's studio. "Well," said Chava again, "then he kissed her on both cheeks. It was embarrassing. He's a funny little man, like a monkey with a black velvet beret, and a kind of smock thing on. Then his wife came in, and he jumped away from Mimi, and told his wife about me—that is, us—wanting our photograph taken. Then he said all kinds of rubbish about how beautiful I was, and how if all my sisters were like me, the photograph would be the toast of Jerusalem, that it would be a masterpiece, a privilege, and so on and so forth. His wife screwed up her mouth, and just asked if we could pay. Mimi waved her arms about a lot, and Monsieur Gustave went 'Pshaw! Money!' as if to say he didn't care if he were paid or not, and then the wife took out a book and wrote Mimi's name down in it, and Monsieur Gustave rushed around the room, picking things up and putting them down, and muttering about finding the right background."

"Was it a very grand place?" asked Rifka.

"Grand? No, not really. Lots of screens with trees and flowers painted on them. A whole collection of potted plants, vases, tables and chairs, little statues, fur rugs, Turkish rugs, things like that. I couldn't find the Gluckmann vase, though. Probably nothing Monsieur Gustave had was good enough for them, and they brought their own vase with them."

Naomi lay back on her bed. "It will be lovely. I shall count the days. I shall make a chart of every hour, and cross each hour off as it passes."

"Perhaps," said Rifka "looking forward to next week will help take my mind away from the thought of Thursday. It's only three days away, and already I'm trembling and hot and cold when I think of it."

"Think of what?" said Naomi.

"Silly! That's when she's going with Mother to visit the Levinskys," said Chava.

38

"Aren't we invited?" said Naomi.

"Are you mad? The Levinskys would take one look at all five of us, and promptly change their minds about the marriage."

"I don't see why," muttered Naomi. "They'll have to meet us sooner or later."

"Later is better," said Chava firmly. "Preferably when it's too late. After all, how embarrassing if David Levinsky falls in love with me, instead of Rifka." She giggled. Tears sprang into Rifka's eyes.

"I've thought of that as well, don't worry. You're so much prettier, and lively and clever, and you always have something ready in your mouth to say. What do I do if he does fall in love with you?"

Chava ran to her sister, and hugged her.

"Oh, Rifka, what nonsense! I'm sorry, sorry, sorry I ever said it. It was only a joke, truly. You are lovely, everyone knows that. No-one would prefer a chatterbox like me, when just to look at you they can see what a good and wonderful person you are. Of course he'll love you. I just hope he's good enough for you."

"I just hope," said Rifka "that he'll know what to say. If he starts, then I think I could continue. But what if he's shy?"

"Then you'll both be quiet and shy together," said Naomi. "There's nothing wrong with that."

"You can borrow my pink ribbon if you like," said Chava. "It'll go nicely with the dress."

"I don't feel like me in that dress," said Rifka. "I wish I could go in my apron, not all that frilly muslin."

"But it looks lovely on you," said Chava. "Don't worry. It'll all go perfectly, I'm sure. And you're to remember every detail about everything to tell us when you get home: what everyone said, and wore, and what you ate, and what the house is like: everything."

Rifka laughed. "I'll never be able to remember it all, and you know I can't describe things properly. In any case, I'll be too nervous to notice."

"Don't dare not to notice," said Naomi. "Mother says they're quite rich, so you must tell us especially what the ladies are wearing."

"What I've been wondering is . . ." said Chava, "if they're so rich, why do they want anything to do with us. Not even a dowry among the five of us."

Rifka lowered her voice, and looked over her shoulder to make sure that her mother was still in the kitchen. "I'll tell you a secret. There *is* a dowry. For all of us. Father left some money when he died, just for that. He'd been saving all his life since we were born. Even the money Grandfather Bernstein left went towards our dowries. He made Mother promise never to use it for anything else."

"I never knew that," Chava breathed. "Well, for my part, I wish they'd take my dowry and buy us all some new clothes."

"And I could use mine to go to America with," said Naomi.

Rifka frowned. "But you're not even supposed to know about it. Promise you won't breathe a word?"

"Very well," said Chava, "although I must admit, it does seem a shame, and I didn't know Mother told you special secrets, just because you're the eldest."

"It's not because of that," said Rifka. "She only told me when the arrangement with the Levinskys was made. Mr. Levinsky thought Father was a very learned and scholarly man, and admired him very much."

"He probably wouldn't have enjoyed living with him, though, any more than we did," said Chava. "Always having to tiptoe about, and not disturb his studies, hardly speaking to him."

Her two sisters looked shocked. "But he was our father, and he's dead," said Naomi. "You shouldn't talk of him like that."

40

"Why not? Just because a person is your father, is the truth not still the truth? I don't see why everyone has to change everything, to make things better all the time, different . . ."

Rifka said: "But what you knew of him, what all of us knew, was only part of the truth. I can remember, when I was very small, being kept awake by his laughter at night. His friends used to come to the house. I don't know why they stopped coming. Once, I remember, he took me and Isaac for a walk. You were still a baby, Chava, and Naomi wasn't even born. He carried me on his shoulders, and picked poppies and cornflowers for me, and called me his little queen. And he sang. I'm quite sure I remember him singing." She wound a strand of hair absent-mindedly around a finger, and smiled.

"By the time I grew up," said Chava, "his walking and singing days were over. And I've got a secret, too, only you must promise *never* to tell."

"We promise," whispered Rifka and Naomi. "Tell us." They huddled together, and Chava said:

"Mimi told me once, and made me promise not to tell, but I'm sure she'd forgive me if she knew I'd told you."

"Don't be so slow," said Naomi. "Tell."

"Well, Mimi said that when Father and Mother's marriage was arranged, the young people weren't allowed to choose at all. You married whoever your parents told you to marry, and that was that. The secret is that Mother never wanted to marry Father, and didn't like him a bit. In fact, Mimi says there was another young man Mother loved at the time, but Grandfather Isaac would not have his name mentioned in the house, and would certainly never consider allowing his daughter to marry him."

Naomi frowned. "But does that mean that Father and Mother didn't love each other?"

"I asked Mimi that," said Chava, "and she said that they grew to

41

love one another in the end, but that Mother was very quiet for the first few months of her marriage."

Sarah's daughters sat in silence for a moment, thinking of their mother in love with someone who was not their father, trying to imagine what she was like when she was young and not succeeding. At last, Rifka said:

"I'm glad I don't have to marry him if I don't want to."

"Yes," said Chava, "and make sure they don't try to persuade you, with promises of money and clothes and things like that. Perhaps you'd better not notice the house too much, and just concentrate on David so that you can tell us exactly what he's like."

"I wonder," said Naomi, "why nobody arranged a marriage for Mimi?"

"Oh, but they tried," said Chava "and only called off the arrangement when she locked herself in her room and refused to talk to anyone, or eat or anything. She was in that room for three days, she told me, and became so ill from it that she had to go abroad with an aunt of hers to recover her strength. They never bothered to arrange a match for her again."

"Maybe she'll marry this Max person you told us about," said Naomi.

"Maybe," Chava yawned, "but I don't think so. She seemed a little sad today for a few minutes, about being all alone, as she put it, but it was soon over. All this talking has made me tired, suddenly. Let's go to sleep now."

"Yes," said Rifka. "I promised Mother we wouldn't talk for long. It must be terribly late."

"The moon is shining right in my face. I'll never sleep, I just know it," murmured Naomi, and fell asleep almost at once.

Chava chuckled, and turned to the wall. "It would take more than a moon to keep me awake tonight. Goodnight, Rifka, and don't worry."

42

"No," said Rifka. "I won't worry. Goodnight, Chava."

The night was so quiet that Rifka could hear her sisters breathing. Outside, the black shapes of the houses were rimmed with silver. Let me like him, thought Rifka, let me be able to like him, and please, God, please let him like me. She leaned her elbows on the windowsill, and looked out of the window again, following with her eyes the silver thread of the street as it wound down the hill and into the darkness.

Chapter IV

"And make sure," said Sarah, "that the little ones have something to eat, if we are late coming home, and watch that they don't run out of the courtyard and down the hill. Dvora is a little devil when it comes to things like that, and Shoshie simply follows."

"Yes, Mother, don't worry," said Chava, feeling very grown-up and responsible. "We'll look after them beautifully. Naomi will tell them stories, and I'll draw them funny pictures, and they'll be with us all the time. You enjoy yourselves."

Rifka managed a rather wobbly smile. For the last twenty minutes she had been sitting at the table, waiting, while Sarah fussed around the room giving last-minute instructions.

"Now, we're ready to go, I think," said Sarah, and kissed her daughters goodbye as if she and Rifka were setting out on a long and perilous journey.

Rifka followed her mother down the steps. Sarah was walking slowly in her good, leather shoes which were stiff and uncomfortable and hurt her feet. She was wearing her best black dress and all the jewellery she owned: a garnet brooch in the shape of a star, and a gold necklace. Around her shoulders, in spite of the heat, was a lace shawl, and on her hands, black lace gloves. Behind her, Rifka looked pale in her pretty muslin dress, her plaits (with Chava's ribbon twined into them) fastened in a crown around her head instead of hanging down her back. Chava, Naomi, Dvora and Shoshie stood on the balcony to wave goodbye. As soon as

44

Sarah and Rifka had vanished out of sight, Dvora and Shoshie began to tug at Naomi's skirt.

"He's gone," Dvora shouted, "gone to visit his grandmother. I heard Mrs. Friedman say. It's safe now. Can we go and stroke the rabbits? Now? Please?"

"I suppose so," said Naomi. "You might as well go and do it at once, or there'll be no peace for the rest of the afternoon."

The little girls ran down the steps and across the courtyard. Naomi and Chava watched them kneeling beside the hutch, their curly brown heads close together.

"That's the house," said Sarah, a little out of breath from the walk, and the long, sloping street they had climbed to reach the Levinskys. Rifka looked, and saw a whitewashed square building, with thick walls and a heavy wooden door, standing in the shade of pine trees and cypress trees.

"Are there other families living here, too?" Rifka asked.

"No, just them, but of course, his mother and father live with them, and their daughter only left last year when she married."

"Still," said Rifka, "it's very large for one family, and a small family, too. What do they find to do in all the rooms?"

"Well, everyone has his own room, I should think, and then perhaps, let's see: a dining-room, and a drawing room, and maybe also a sewing room, and a kitchen, and a guest bedroom, and a room to bath in." Sarah counted them on her fingers.

"Why can't they bath in the kitchen? It seems silly to have a whole room, just for that."

"Well, at least it means that you can cook the evening meal without being splashed, or slipping to your death on a cake of soap."

Plumbago bushes, heavy with pale blue flowers, grew in stone urns on either side of the door. Rifka and her mother stood for a moment, glancing about them. Sarah looked at her daughter. She smoothed Rifka's hair, and wiped a trace of dust from her cheek with a small handkerchief.

"There, now you look perfect. I'm going to ring the bell."

"Yes," said Rifka, and took a deep breath. I've never known what it meant till now, she thought, wanting the earth to open, and swallow you up, but now I know, oh, I know, and I wish it would. Sarah pulled at the iron handle of the bell, and Rifka heard it echoing dully somewhere far away inside the house. A few seconds—an eternity of seconds—went by, and then the door opened.

"Mrs. Bernstein! And Rifka! How lovely! Come, come in. You must both be half dead from the heat."

Rifka stepped into the cool room behind her mother, and looked at the lady who was perhaps, one day to be her mother-in-law. Her voice was clear and pleasant, and she herself was tall and handsome, with a figure that could only just escape being described as fat. Her dress, Rifka noted for her sisters' benefit, was plum-coloured silk embroidered with jet beads, and she wore a jet necklace, and had her hair swept up into an intricate arrangement of stiff, iron-grey curls on top of her head. She smiled a lot, perhaps a little too much, as she talked to Sarah, showing a great many very straight, shiny teeth.

"And this is Rifka, it must be," she said, as if she had just made a pleasant and surprising discovery. "You look lovely, child, just as lovely as they said you were."

They? Who said I was? Rifka blushed, and muttered: "Thank you," and tried to find traces of insincerity in Mrs. Levinsky's face, but she looked as if she meant every word. Perhaps she does, thought Rifka. Chava is always telling me I should believe the nice things people say about me. But who could have told her? I wonder if she knows the Gluckmanns? Maybe she buys cakes at the bakery.

"Come with me on to the balcony, and meet the family. We've all been waiting so long for this visit." They made their way through many rooms, it seemed to Rifka, with high ceilings and white walls. Turkish rugs lay on the tiled floors, and Rifka watched her own familiar, brown shoes treading on strange, rich blues and reds, and leaves, and branches full of white birds, and borders of squares and triangles in yellow and black and green, and tasselled fringes of scarlet silk.

The balcony, when they reached it, was like no other balcony that Rifka had ever seen. It was a small room, with a ceiling and two walls made of wooden trellis-work, thickly covered in vines. Bunches of grapes, almost black, and dusted with a fine white bloom hung down from the diamond-shaped holes overhead. There was no fourth wall, and in a frame of translucent green vine leaves, the red-brown hills fell away to the horizon. Rifka stopped, looking at an olive tree in the distance which she had chosen because she had not dared to look at the people sitting on cane chairs in the flickering, green shadows. I could just run away into that garden and down the hill, she thought wildly. But there was nowhere to go now, no way of escaping. Mrs. Levinsky held her elbow and gently pushed her forward into the centre of the group.

"Sarah Bernstein you already know, of course", she said, "but this is Rifka, her eldest daughter. Rifka, these are our Grandmother and Grandfather Levinsky, my husband Moshe, my sister-in-law Zipporah and her husband, Chaim, and this is David. There, now apart from my daughter, who lives in Tiberias, you've met the whole family."

Mimi was lying on her bed in a pale pink crêpe-de-chine peignoir. Beside her on the table was a small bowl of salted almonds, another filled with Turkish Delight, and a peach on a white saucer.

Her novel lay open on the pillow, and she was thinking of Rifka, at this very minute, probably, meeting her young man for the first time. Poor child. Please God, let her be happy. "Marriage is a lottery," said Mimi, aloud, quite surprising herself by the profundity of her thought. Either you win or you lose. What shall I wear to play cards at Ruhama's later? The coffee-coloured lace, I think. Ruhama's skin can't take the colour. She may be covered head to foot in emeralds, but my complexion she hasn't got. Mimi picked up the peach, and began to cut slices from it with a silver knife. She ate them daintily, licking the juice from her fingers after each bite.

"What are you doing?" Naomi asked from her place in the middle of a pile of cushions on the sofa.

"Reading," said Chava, "and I've nearly finished this bit, so don't talk to me."

"Alright. Sorry." Then, almost to herself: "I wonder where the little ones are. Perhaps I'd better go and see. They're very quiet."

Chava was silent. She's not saying anything, thought Naomi, but I can see from her back that she wishes I would go away, or find something to do. I wonder what Rifka is feeling now. She must have met him by this time. I hope he's very handsome. I wonder if he'll fall in love with her as soon as he sees her, like in the stories. Where are Dvora and Shoshie? They're very quiet. I'd better go and see. Naomi pulled herself out of the cushions and went out on to the balcony. There was no-one beside the rabbit hutch, no-one in the courtyard. Naomi felt a little sick. They've gone down the hill, she thought, they've run away. Oh, God, let them be safe! What will Mother say if they're lost? Naomi shuddered. I must tell Chava, she thought, she'll know what to do. She ran into the dining-room shouting: "Chava, come quickly, come! I can't find the little ones. They've disappeared. They're not by the hutch any more. I'm sure they've run away. Oh, Chava, please come. What are we going to do?"

"Have you looked for them?" said Chava, closing her book with a worried frown.

"No, I came to find you as soon as I saw they weren't in the courtyard."

"Well, we must start looking." Chava rose to her feet. "First, we'll try their room, and our bedroom and the kitchen. They may have come back quietly without telling us."

Chava even looked under the beds, but Dvora and Shosie were nowhere to be found.

"Perhaps the Friedmans invited them in for a drink or a cake?" suggested Naomi.

"With Menahem so horrible to them all the time? I doubt it very much."

The little girls were not at the Friedmans', nor on any of the other balconies.

"Perhaps they're hiding somewhere," said Chava, who was beginning to sound more and more worried.

"Oh, Chava," said Naomi, bursting into tears, "what can have happened to them? What will Mother say?"

Chava shook her head violently, as if to clear it of things too terrible to think about. Then, standing in the middle of the courtyard, she shouted out:

"Dvora! Shoshanna! Come out now! It's time for a cake. Come out, Dvora. Shoshie, where are you?"

Her voice echoed in the drowsy air of the afternoon. Nothing. No Dvora. No Shoshie. She tried again. Naomi was sobbing now, crouching on the paving-stones with her face hidden in her apron.

"Dvora! Shoshanna! Come out now. Come home. We've got something lovely for you."

The door of the Old Man's room creaked open, and suddenly,

there they were. Chava watched them running towards her: giggling, running and alive. That was the main thing, thought Chava. Nothing had happened to them. Naomi looked up, and gave a shout of pure relief. She wiped her face, and stood up. Almost immediately, the two elder girls began shouting. Chava yelled:

"What were you doing, hiding like that? You're naughty and disobedient."

"You're supposed to tell us where you are. We were worried to death."

"Why were you disturbing the poor Old Man? I expect he wanted to sleep, and you stopped him."

"He didn't," said Dvora, complacently. "He told us it was kind of us to come, because no-one visits him. He let us look at his picture book."

"What picture book?" said Chava. "I don't believe he even has a picture book."

"He has. It's a Hagadah, like the one we use for Passover, only it has pictures of all the ten plagues that God sent, in colours. Lovely pictures of Boils and Frogs, and Darkness, and Lice, and Death of the Firstborn, and everything."

"But you're too little to understand all that," said Chava.

"No, the Old Man told us the whole story. It was very exciting. Moses made God send the Plagues, so that Pharoah would let the people of Israel leave Egypt, where they were being treated not nicely at all." Dvora looked pleased with herself.

"Well, all the same," said Chava, "you should have come and told us where you were. Come upstairs now and have something to eat."

"How did you understand what the Old Man was saying?" asked Naomi.

"Well," said Dvora, "I had to listen very hard, and then I

understood, and I explained to Shoshie. Don't you think that was nice of me?"

"I suppose it was," sighed Chava. "I suppose so."

"What was the something lovely you said you had for us?" asked Dvora.

"Something lovely you want, do you, after that naughty behaviour? You be grateful I'm not Moses, because if I were, I'd ask for a few special plagues for you."

Dvora was silent, pondering. Then she said: "I think I'd like Frogs best of all, but if not Frogs, then I wouldn't mind Locusts. D'you think God would do it for you, if you asked him?"

" . . . and when Shoshanna, my youngest, was born, and I was ill for a month, Rifka did everything for the baby," said Sarah, and smiled round at the grave, approving faces of the Levinsky family.

"Yes," said Mrs. Levinsky, "it's quite clear to see that Rifka would make a wonderful mother. David, would you pass Rifka a slice of the cinnamon cake, please? She's hardly touched a thing."

"Won't eat a husband out of house and home," chuckled Mr. Levinsky. His wife frowned at him, then summoned a new white smile on to her features again, to display to the others.

"And what do you hear from your daughter in Tiberias?" said Sarah, aware suddenly of the silence, knowing that the topic of Rifka's excellence had been fully explored.

Rifka let out a long breath. She felt as though she had been holding herself together in a tight bundle ever since she had sat down, and only now that the talk had become more general did she dare raise her eyes from the legs of the cane table, which she had been examining for what seemed like hours. There was David. After all the thinking and imagining and picturing how he would look, he was just an ordinary boy, with bony wrists sticking out of his white sleeves, and a thin, rather sad face, and dark, soft hair. I won't be able to tell them he's handsome, thought Rifka. Chava will say I told you so, and Naomi will be upset that he isn't a prince, nor even as handsome as Isaac. He looks worried. Perhaps he always does, or perhaps it's just being faced with me. Poor Mr. Levinsky is scared of his wife. His hands shook a little when she handed him his teacup, as if he were not used to fine china. His fingers are fat and clumsy, but he seems kind. At least he tried to make a joke. She didn't like that. The grandmother is asleep. She opened her eyes to look at me when I came, and then fell asleep again. No-one even bothers to pour her a cup of tea. There is a samovar from the Old Country, from Russia, on the cane table, and at least four kinds of cake. The grandfather is reading. Not a heavy prayerbook, nor a Talmud, but a small book with a yellow paper cover and letters in French, or English. Mr. Levinsky's sister is smartly dressed, but she has an unpleasant face with eyes too close together, and a lot of hair on her upper lip. This doesn't seem to worry her husband, who springs up every five minutes and puts another cake on her plate. He is obviously devoted to her.

" . . . a beautiful villa by the lake. They find it so healthy for the baby," said Mrs. Levinsky.

"It is a lovely place," said Sarah. "I went there once with my dear late husband, and my son, before any of the girls were born. I still remember how pleasant it was, dipping my feet in the water."

"Biarritz," said the old grandfather suddenly. "You haven't lived till you've been to Biarritz."

"Yes, Father, Biarritz is lovely," said his daughter-in-law in the sort of voice used to placate children, but the old man had taken up his book and was no longer listening.

"Perhaps," said Sarah, "in the spring, you would all come on a picnic with us? We have a favourite spot we often go to, and a friend lends us his mule-cart."

Oh, no, Rifka screamed inwardly, no, no, no! Can't she see that these are not picnic people, not mule-cart people? She waited for a polite refusal, but to her surprise, Mrs. Levinsky clapped her hands, and exclaimed joyfully:

"Oh, yes, how lovely! We'd love that, wouldn't we, Moshe? Thank you so much. I haven't been on a picnic for years. You'd like that, David, wouldn't you?"

"Yes," said David, so quietly that Rifka could scarcely hear him, "that would be very nice."

"Pâté is for picnics," said the grandfather. "Pâté de foie gras." Mrs. Levinsky laughed nervously.

"Naughty Father! What will Mrs. Bernstein think? You know pâté isn't Kosher."

"It's delicious, though," said the grandfather. "You don't know what you're missing." He chuckled and wheezed into the pages of his book.

"He's very old," said Mrs. Levinsky to Sarah in an apologetic whisper. "I'm afraid his youth was a little, well, raffish, shall we say." She leaned closer to Sarah, and said, confidingly, in an even lower voice: "He led my mother-in-law quite a dance in his day. Oh, yes, quite a dance. He was extremely handsome, of course. Not that I think that's any excuse."

Rifka was fascinated. She looked at the bent little man with the white beard and the bald head, the lined, sagging cheeks and the thin-lipped, nearly toothless mouth, and tried to imagine him as a handsome young man. As she was staring, he looked up, and met her eyes, and smiled. She turned away, but not before the old man had winked at her—yes, unmistakably winked at her. His eyes were blue, and still very bright. Perhaps, after all, it was not hard to imagine how charming he must have been.

"Who are these people?" The grandmother spoke these words into the silence that had fallen. Immediately, her son and her daughter fussed around her, gathering up her shawl, and muttering comforting words about resting, and lying down inside, and the heat being too much for her. The old lady was led away into the house.

"Poor Mother," said Mrs. Levinsky, who had not moved from her chair to help the old lady, "she is a little deaf, and so misses a great deal of what goes on. But she is our dearest Mother and we all love her. David is devoted to her, aren't you, my dear?"

"Yes," said David again, and pulled his shirt cuffs down to hide his wrists.

"David." The grandfather put his book aside, and groped for his stick. Painfully, slowly, he stood up.

"Yes, Grandfather," said the boy.

"They've brought this girl here to see if you would like her as a bride. Am I right? Don't shush me, Panya, I'm not talking to you. Well, am I right?"

"Yes, Grandfather," said David, blushing all over. Even his hands were crimson. Rifka felt herself reddening, too.

"Then what are the two of you doing, sitting there like two turnips? Listening to a lot of boring talk. Take the girl, and show her the garden, and get to know her properly." Turning to go, he waved and said: "Do it now, boy, before they freeze you to your chair with all their chit-chat. Goodbye. I'm going now." He left the room, giggling into his beard. Everyone began to talk at once, to smooth over the old gentleman's breach of etiquette. David and Rifka sat on their chairs, and looked at one another directly for the first time. David smiled, and rose to his feet. He went over to where Rifka was sitting, and stood in front of her. She looked down at his shoes, concentrating hard on how very shiny they were.

"Miss Bernstein . . . er . . . Rifka, would you like to see our garden?" David spoke in a whisper.

"Thank you very much," said Rifka, and her voice felt as though it were coming from a long way away. "That would be lovely."

Together, they went down the steps that led from the balcony into the garden.

With the shutters half-closed, Mimi thought, and at this distance from the mirror, I still look good. If I half-shut my eyes, the shadowy figure over there could be me, if not aged twenty, then thirty, perhaps? Certainly forty. What will Max think of me? Will he notice the lines on my face? He'll no longer be able to span my waist in his two hands. I'm nervous, like a young girl. What will we talk about? Stupid. He's an old man now, Max. Will there be anything of him left to recognise? Mimi picked up a comb, and began to twist curls into place around her brow. She fastened a cameo brooch at the neck of the coffee-coloured lace dress, and opened the crystal bottle of heliotrope perfume. The fragrance of warm gardens at night. Will Max's memories be the same as mine, Mimi wondered, replacing the bottle on the chest of drawers. I don't believe any two people remember anything in the same way. Shared memories are a lot of novelettish nonsense. Mimi threw a black silk shawl around her shoulders. She was ready for an evening of canasta with friends who all looked, most gratifyingly, a great deal older than she did herself.

"And one day," said Naomi, "the most exciting thing happened."

"What?" said Dvora.

"Eat your fish and I'll tell you. And you, Shoshie."

"I'll cut it up smaller for you," said Chava, who was sitting on the other side of Shoshie at the table.

"What exciting thing?" said Dvora.

"Well, it was decided . . . the king decided that the eldest princess had to be married."

"Is that exciting? I don't think that's very exciting." Dvora pushed pieces of fish around her plate. "Do you think its exciting, Shoshie?"

"Don't know," said Shoshie, who was quite enjoying her meal, now that kind Chava was feeding her to save time, and she didn't have to concentrate on keeping her spoon full of fish until it reached her mouth.

"Well, I *do* know," said Naomi, "it was very exciting because all the young princes from far and wide had to have a competition to see who was the best prince of all."

"Why?" asked Dvora.

"Because only the very best prince in the world would be good enough for the princess."

"Why? I don't understand." Dvora frowned.

Naomi sighed. "Because the princess was so very good and beautiful and clever that the king and queen knew that only a very special prince would do for her, so they held all sorts of competitions to find the best prince. Now do you understand?"

"Yes," said Dvora.

"No," said Shoshie.

"Don't worry, Naomi," Dvora smiled. "I'll tell her about that later. Tell about the competitions."

"Yes, I will, but first, let me give you your apricots." She put glass dishes of apricots stewed in sugar and lemon juice in front of the little girls. This was their favourite sweet, and Chava sat back gratefully while Shoshie attacked the slippery fruit with great enthusiasm and much spilling of juice on the table-cloth and on the front of her dress. Naomi sat down and continued the story.

"Now, the competitions. Let's see. There was a running competition. The princes had to run up and down a very steep hill twenty times."

"How silly," said Dvora. "What for?"

Naomi thought for a moment. "To show that they were strong and healthy."

"Mother says milk makes you strong and healthy."

"It does," Chava interrupted. "The prince who won was the one who had drunk gallons of it when he was a boy. Isn't that so, Naomi?"

"Of course," said Naomi, a little vexed at Chava's interruption. "Then they had a competition to see who could kill the most dragons."

"Why?" asked Dvora.

"To see who was the bravest and most fearless, naturally. The princess would never marry a coward."

"I think they should have a competition to see who can bring the princess the best present," said Dvora.

"That's a good idea," said Naomi. "They did have that competition, to show who was the kindest and most generous. And the princes brought jewels, and gold, and crowns thickly studded with pearls, and silks, and chests full of coins, but none of them won the prize."

"Who won, then?" asked Dvora.

"The prince who brought an orange tree in a tub, with two nightingales sitting on the branches."

"That's stupid. I'm sure the princess would rather have had jewels. I would," said Dvora. "Are there any more apricots?"

"Yes, in a minute. You're being silly, Dvora. Jewels and things can get lost or broken. A tree lasts forever, because from the fruit you can plant more trees. And the nightingales would have baby nightingales, and so that would go on for ever, too, even after the prince and princess were dead."

"If they were dead, then they wouldn't care if the tree grew or not."

"It's difficult to explain," Naomi said. "Chava, do you understand?"

"Yes, I understand," said Chava, "although Dvora does have a point, you know."

Shoshie smiled. "I understand, too. The princess liked oranges for eating, like me."

"Yes," said Naomi, "she did. You're a clever little kitten, Shoshie. She loved oranges for breakfast."

"It was the same prince who won the running and the dragon-killing and the kindness prize, wasn't it, Naomi? By a lucky co-incidence."

Naomi stuck out her tongue. "Not a coincidence at all, Chava dear. It always happens like that in stories, so there."

They walked in silence along the stony path which led down the hill through a short avenue of trees. Leaves hung motionless and dusty-green on dry branches, and as they walked, Rifka noticed her carefully polished shoes clouding over with yellow dust. I must say something, she thought, anything. What shall I say? Will I seem forward of me? But we can't walk along like this in silence. The garden. I'll say how lovely it is. I'll just open my mouth now and say 'This is a really lovely garden.' It won't be hard at all.

"I'm afraid the garden looks terrible," said David, looking sideways at her, and then frowning.

"No, it's lovely. I was just going to say what a lovely garden it is."

"Really? It's all dried up now. In summer, you know, it's all dry and brown, but in the spring, well, all these trees here have blossoms. Peaches, almonds, plums, apricots."

"Where is the fruit then? Surely there should be fruit?"

"We picked it just last week. I wish . . ." David frowned again,

58

and fell silent.

"What do you wish?" Rifka trembled at her own daring. David looked at her.

"I wish you could have seen it all, lying in the baskets. That's all."

"I wish I had, too. Sometimes I find it hard to believe that things in the market used to be on the trees."

"Next year, you can come and see the blossom. And the fruit," said David, and began to walk on down the path. Rifka followed him, nearly running to keep up. Next year. He wants me to see it all next year. It means he likes me. Or maybe he's just being polite. She sighed. How difficult it is to know what someone else is really thinking.

They reached a clearing of recently-dug earth at the bottom of the avenue, where slabs of sandstone, gold and faintly pink in the late afternoon sunlight, were neatly stacked one on top of another in small piles.

"Come and sit down," said David, "on these stones, and I'll show you what the garden is going to be like."

Rifka sat down carefully.

"It's my mother's idea," David continued. "It used to be beautiful here. Wild cyclamen in spring, and poppies in the summer, and marigolds and oleander bushes. But now she's going to make a terrace with stone urns and flower-beds all around and I think she even has ideas of a fountain, or maybe a pool with goldfish."

"It sounds very grand," said Rifka.

"Yes, but it was wild before. I liked it like that." He turned to face her. "Did you mind what Grandfather said? Did it make you feel embarrassed? I'm sorry if it did."

"No, not really. I didn't mind at all. I like him."

"Do you? I'm so glad. The rest think he's like a very old naughty child, but he tells such marvellous stories. And when I was small,

59

he always had things in his pockets for me that I wasn't supposed to have: sugared almonds and things like that."

"Turkish Delight," said Rifka.

David smiled. "Yes, that's right. How do you know?"

"I have an aunt that's the same as your grandfather, a little. My mother disapproves of her."

David nodded, and immediately Rifka wondered if she had said too much. After all, she hardly knew David. Was it right to tell him private things about her family?

"Tell me about your sisters," he said, almost as if he knew what she was thinking.

"Chava is next after me. She's eleven, and she's clever. And very pretty. She wants to study to be something like a doctor or a scientist, but I don't know how she will. Then comes Naomi. She's eight. She's forgetful, and makes up poems and stories. She believes everything you tell her and everything she reads. Chava teases her and she hates that. Dvora is five. She's tidy and bossy and stubborn, and she has big, blue eyes, and curly hair. She's very proud of her hair, because she's the only one of us with curls. Shoshanna is sweet. She's only three, and she has fat little legs and arms, and a round face with a dimple when she smiles, and a fringe." Rifka stopped suddenly. "I'm sorry. It must be boring for you. I'm talking too much."

"No, go on. It's very interesting. My sister is so much older than me, it's almost like having two mothers. I wish I had someone near my own age, to talk to."

"We quarrel sometimes," said Rifka, to make him feel better, "and if you're older, you have to do quite a lot of work, too."

"Still, it sounds as if you could never be lonely."

"No, that's true. But also, you're never alone. Chava, Naomi and I share a room, you see."

"It's not so nice to be alone," said David.

"No," said Rifka, "no, I can see that. I wouldn't really like it."

David said: "I hope I meet them all soon. I'd like to see them."

Rifka blushed. What was she supposed to say? She took a deep breath. "I'll ask my mother. Perhaps you could all visit us one day."

"Yes, I hope so. Will your aunt be there? The one you told me about?"

"Well, I don't think so. She doesn't come very often. I hope . . ." Rifka's voice faltered.

"What were you going to say?"

"I mean, I hope you aren't expecting anything very grand. We only live in a tiny place. And we have neighbours all around, not like your house," Rifka mumbled.

"Where you live," said David, very slowly and carefully, not looking at Rifka, "doesn't matter. It doesn't matter at all."

Rifka bent down and brushed some imaginary dirt from the hem of her dress, so that David should not see her confusion. Did he mean it as she understood it? That he liked her so much that he didn't care about where she lived, it would make no difference to his feelings? Or maybe he meant that he simply didn't care about things like people's houses in general? I must remember to ask Chava. And Mimi. Mimi will know if it means that he likes me.

"We should go back now, I think," David said, and stood up. He stretched out his hand to Rifka, and in a kind of dumb trance she gave him her hand and rose from her pile of stones. He'll let go now, she thought, he only took my hand to help me up. His hand is dry and strong. I can feel the bones. Why is my hand so damp? Oh, please, let him not let go of my hand.

"Come," said David, and pulled her gently towards the path. Oh, yes, we are, thought Rifka, we are. We are going to walk right up to the house, and he'll hold my hand all the way. He must like me. I'm sure that means he likes me. I'm growing used to it now, but it feels different. I've always held hands with the little ones, but it doesn't feel the same at all. I feel as if my whole inside is melting away. Why is that? Does it mean that I like him? I haven't even thought about it. She looked sideways at David, who was staring with great concentration at a point some inches in front of his shoes. He turned to her suddenly and smiled.

I do like him, Rifka thought with a sudden warm feeling of happiness. Yes I do. He has a lovely smile.

"I'll ask Mother for a basket of peaches for you," he said. "And for your mother and sisters, of course."

"It's very kind of you," said Rifka, smiling too.

"Next year," said David, "you'll see how it looks with all the blossom."

As they approached the balcony, David let go of Rifka's hand.

Mimi and the other ladies had stopped playing cards, and were drinking coffee and eating cakes specially baked to be the size of one mouthful. Silly cakes, thought Mimi. You have to eat ten before you feel you've had anything. Ruhama was holding forth on the subject of marriage. My fault, Mimi told herself. I should never have gossiped about Rifka and the Levinsky boy.

"In my opinion," Ruhama was saying, brushing crumbs from her maroon taffeta bosom, "young people can't possibly know what they want. Parents are the ones most capable of making wise choices for their children. Imagine if everyone were allowed to choose! So many totally unsuitable marriages."

"You're talking nonsense, Ruhama," said Mimi, laughing, "and as for your memory, you've lost it altogether. Who cried all the way through the wedding ceremony, and for three months afterwards?"

"But," said Ruhama with dignity, "I haven't forgotten at all. I grew to love my husband, as my parents knew I would. I'm eternally grateful to them. Eliezer is the best of men."

And lavish with the gemstones, Mimi thought, but she only said: "Well, I still believe in love. I've always believed in it, and I still do."

Ruhama smiled. I know what you're thinking, Mimi said to herself, as she smiled sweetly back. You're thinking that all my belief in love hasn't brought me a husband and children. Well, my dear, there's more to life than a husband and children. There's fun, and travel, and meeting people, and being my own mistress, and that's more than you'll ever know, tied to an old crock like Eliezer, never allowed to move without his permission. And which of us looks better, Mimi asked herself privately, and was pleased with the answer.

"Shall we play another hand?" Ruhama suggested. "I think we have time."

The ladies gathered round the table again. As Ruhama dealt the cards, Mimi leaned towards her, and said in a confiding whisper:

"One of my old beaux from France, Maximilian von Eschenloer, is visiting me very soon. Did I tell you?"

"No, you didn't," said Ruhama. "I'm sorry, ladies, I shall have to deal this hand again. I'm afraid I've not been concentrating properly."

That's given her something to ponder, thought Mimi with satisfaction, watching the diamonds twinkling on Ruhama's fingers as she gathered up the cards.

"But I want to wait till Mother and Rifka come home," said Dvora. "Why can't I?"

"Because," said Chava, "it's late. Shoshie is already asleep, look, and now it's time for you to go to sleep, too."

"I want a drink."

"You've had a drink."

63

"But it's hot. I want another drink."

"I'll get you some water and then," said Chava sternly, "we won't have you being hungry, or feeling sick, or wanting another story or lullaby or anything."

"But I *am* hungry, and I *do* want another story," said Dvora.

"You've eaten enough to last a week," said Chava, "and Naomi is washing your plates from supper, and she's told you a story already."

"You tell me one then."

"You know I can't," said Chava. "I don't know how to make things up."

"You could tell a real story," said Dvora cunningly.

"Yes," said Chava, "I could, and I won't, except for this story: Once upon a time there was a little girl who went to sleep so late that her sister woke up hours before her in the morning, and went to feed the rabbits all on her own."

"Is that supposed to be me and Shoshie?" asked Dvora.

"Yes, you old silly, of course it is. Now, come on, lie down, and I'll fetch you your drink, and then you can go straight to sleep."

Dvora sighed. "Alright. I suppose so."

Chava went out to fetch the water, and Dvora lay in bed determined to keep her eyes open until Rifka and Mother came home. I'll listen for them coming up the stairs, and then I'll pretend they woke me up coming up the stairs making a noise and talking as they were coming up the stairs, and then I'll get out of bed and pretend I was asleep all the time, and they just woke me up that minute and I'll pretend that I wasn't waiting for them to come home, and that I was asleep all the time.

Chava, coming in with a glass of water, found Dvora with her eyes closed and her curls falling around her neck. Her mouth was a little open, and she was breathing deeply and evenly. Chava put the glass down on the chest of drawers. Little minx, she is, she thought, laughing to herself as she lifted Dvora's hair away from her neck, and looked around for a ribbon to tie it with. I should have plaited it before, she thought. Now the poor little thing will dream she's all bundled up in a fur coat. She kissed Dvora on the cheek, and went out on to the balcony. Naomi was sitting on the top step, waiting.

"Surely they should be back by now, Chava, shouldn't they?" She sounded worried.

"It's only seven o'clock. It's early. They're probably having a marvellous time. And it's a long way to walk, all the way to Yemin Moshe and back."

"Yes, but I wish they'd come. I want to know what happened."

"You'll know, soon enough. And don't start jumping around asking idiotic questions when they come."

"I don't ask idiotic questions."

"You do sometimes."

"They're not idiotic."

"Alright, they're not idiotic. But don't ask them anyway. Rifka will tell us when we're in bed. She's not going to say anything in front of Mother."

"There they are! Look! Rifka! Mother, here we are!" Naomi ran down the steps to greet Sarah and Rifka, who were walking slowly into the courtyard.

"Oh Naomi, my child," moaned Sarah, "fetch my slippers, if you love me. My feet are swollen like two I don't know what exactly. Pumpkins, maybe. And hurting, so badly are they hurting I don't think I can even manage the steps."

"Come on, Mother, I'll help you," said Naomi.

"I'm getting the slippers, Mother," said Chava, disappearing into the kitchen.

"What is in the basket?" Naomi asked Rifka, who had been standing silently beside her mother.

"Peaches from the Levinskys' trees," said Rifka.

Naomi's eyes widened. "Have they got orchards?"

"Not orchards. A few fruit trees, that's all."

"But," said Sarah, climbing the stairs painfully with Naomi at her side, "such lovely people. They made us so welcome, and Rifka looked so lovely and behaved so beautifully. Oh, I'm so happy and proud. I wish your father were alive. I'm sure it's a good match."

"Here are the slippers, Mother," said Chava.

Sarah sat down on the top step, and took off her shoes.

"Heaven! Pure heaven! Now my feet feel better. Thank you, Chavale. Rifka, don't just stand there clutching that basket. Put the peaches into the fruit bowl."

"Yes, Mother." Rifka went into the dining-room and began transferring the fruit slowly from the basket to the bowl. Naomi followed her, and watched her sister from the door, longing to rush in and ask a thousand questions. Rifka took the last peach out of the basket. It still had a little twig, and two dried leaves attached to it. Rifka broke the leaves off, and put them carefully into her pocket, before adding the peach to the heap in the fruit bowl. Now why didn't she just throw that away, thought Naomi. She's behaving very strangely. She's hardly said anything. I think it's true love. I'm sure true lovers go about in a dream. I wish it was bedtime, so that we could find out all about him.

"Hello, Naomi." Rifka had turned and seen her standing in the doorway.

"You look lovely," stammered Naomi.

Rifka walked over to her sister and hugged her tightly. "Oh, Naomi, I do love you!"

Naomi hugged Rifka and said: "I love you, too," thinking: she's a little mad. Is that what going to be married is supposed to do?

66

Rifka lay awake for a long time after her sisters had fallen asleep, watching the lamplight from the kitchen make a golden road across the ceiling: narrow near the door and widening as it crossed the room. I've told them everything, she thought, and nothing at the same time. They know all about what we did, what we said, what we ate, what everyone wore, what David looks like, what the house and garden are like, and yet they know nothing. Nothing about how I feel. How do I feel? Strange, not like myself. Will I marry him? Will we still be together when we're old? Have children? Who will they look like? Will David be a good father to them? Where will we live? When will Mother invite them here? Will we have a picnic together in the spring? I don't know any answers. Naomi thought, from what I said, that it was love at first sight, but she would, of course. Chava said she honestly couldn't tell, that it depended on the voice, and the look, and the whole atmosphere, but that it sounded promising. The light is silver now. Mother has carried the lamp into the dining room, and there's only the moonlight left.

Chapter V

"I don't want to wear that dress." Dvora screwed her face up, ready to cry. "I'm not wearing it."

Chava groaned. "But why, Dvora? I can't see why."

"It's dirty. And the hem is broken."

"Down, not broken. You say the hem is down. I can't see where it's dirty. Look, Naomi and Shoshie and I are all wearing the same dress. Don't you want to wear yours too, so that we all look just the same? Rifka would wear hers, only hers is mine now, and mine is Naomi's and she hasn't got one, so she has to wear another dress."

"My dress is dirty and the hem is broken down."

"Just down."

"Just down."

"No, *down*, Dvora. Down. Down. Your hem is down."

"That's right, my hem is down. I told you it was. I'm wearing the dress with the big, white collar. I like the big, white collar bestest of all."

Chava did not bother to correct the mistake. All she said was:

"But where's the dirt?" She looked carefully at the front of the dress. "I can't see it."

"I can't see it as well, but I know it's there. And I'm not wearing that dress."

Rifka was brushing Shoshie's hair. She said: "For goodness sake, Chava, what does it matter? I'm not wearing the same dress. Let her put on whatever she wants, or she'll cry for hours."

Chava took the dress with the big white collar out of the cupboard, and forced Dvora's arms into it rather roughly. Dvora pushed her head out through the neck opening, and smiled at Chava.

"I'm a pretty Dvora now," she said smugly.

"You're stubborn, and spoiled, and silly, and . . ." Chava tried to think of another word beginning with "s" and was just on the point of adding "selfish", when Dvora smiled again and made her smile too. ". . . and very, very pretty," she ended instead, and kissed the top of her little sister's head.

Rifka was standing in front of the mirror, trying to see as much as possible of her dress. It was new, for her, and its previous owner, their mother's cousin's daughter, had only worn it a few times. She stroked the lace panel that stretched from the neck to the waist, and admired the three little buttons, made of real jet, sewn in a diagonal line on to the pocket. And such a colour: blue, like the sky on a spring morning. A great pity, thought Rifka, that the colour would not be seen in the photograph. Feeling a little guilty at having the smartest dress, she said quickly to Chava and Naomi:

"You look very nice, and so do the little ones."

Chava and Naomi, both feeling envious, and yet knowing that this was the only dress Rifka could possibly wear, went over to the mirror to look at themselves.

"Not bad, I suppose," said Chava, "but next year, don't forget, that dress will be mine. Thank goodness you're a fast grower."

"Mine the year after that," said Naomi, "but by then it'll be out of style, the buttons will probably have fallen off, and I'll be so sick of seeing it on you two that it won't feel new at all. My things never do."

"You'll have all your fine dresses when you get to America," said Rifka. "Now, let's hurry and say goodbye to Mother. And if she asks about the clothes, remember to say that Mimi is having guests for lunch. I don't want to be late today, so hurry."

"Why don't you?" asked Dvora.

"Why don't I what?" said Rifka.

"Want to be late today."

"Never mind why," said Chava, "just put on your hats and come along."

"Party?" asked Shoshie. "Is a party?"

"No, little chicken, it's not a party, even though you've got your party dress on. You'll see later. Now, come, let's look for Mother."

The girls found their mother in the courtyard, taking washing off the line, and folding it into a big straw basket.

"We're going now, Mother," said Rifka. "We've just come to say goodbye."

"Good," said Sarah. "Give my regards to Miriam, and tell her I hope she's well, as if a woman like that is ever anything else. And don't be late home, and see that Shoshie eats a proper lunch, if such a thing is possible in that house."

"Yes, Mother, we will. And we won't be late," said Chava. "Do you want us to take the washing upstairs for you before we go?"

"No, no, you go and enjoy yourselves. I'll do it," said Sarah, kissing each of her daughters in turn. The girls went out into the street together. When they had been gone a few minutes, their mother suddenly realised that they had all been wearing their best dresses. Perhaps Miriam was going to take them out somewhere, to a café or somewhere equally unsuitable for children. The woman really was impossible.

Mimi put her hand to her brow and stood looking at the five sisters sitting in a row on her bed.

"It's nearly right, but there's just something . . . something that could be better. Now let's see. The hair. Of course, it's the hair, it must be. Those thick plaits at the back are dreary. Now don't look so offended, dreary is what they are, and dreary is what you'll look if they remain. You must all take out your plaits and brush your hair. It must be loose, and flowing, like a waterfall."

"But we never wear our hair loose, Mimi," Rifka protested. "We even plait it before bed."

"Loose is how you're wearing it today, my darlings. Come, I'll help you brush it."

A little later, Mimi considered the effect once more.

"Lovely!" she announced. "Just right for the present I have for each of you."

"Present! Shoshie want present!" The little girl ran to her aunt, and began to pluck at her skirt.

"Shoshie shall have one, and so shall all the others." Mimi took a parcel wrapped in tissue paper out of a drawer, and with a rustle and a flourish, like a conjurer, produced five lengths of wide, silk ribbon. Naomi spoke first.

"Oh, how lovely! Are they really for us?"

"Yes, one for each of you. Each one a different colour. Royal blue for you, Rifka, turquoise for Chava, yellow for Naomi, mauve for Dvora, and pink for our little rosebud."

The girls took the ribbons, and ran them lovingly through their fingers, and held them up to shimmer in the sunlight, and draped them against their dresses, and rolled them up, and let them unroll again.

"They're for your hair," said Mimi. "I'll pin them on myself."

Chava, Naomi, Dvora and Shoshie were delighted with their bows. Only Rifka said:

"Mimi, I look ridiculous, like a witch at a wedding, or something. Well, don't I?"

71

Everybody looked at Rifka. No one said anything. Then Mimi said: "It's because your hair is so black, and straight and long. Your beauty is more of the classical variety, so for you we will tie the hair behind your ears, like this . . ." and in a moment, there was Rifka, looking not so much like a witch, but more like a pretty schoolteacher, with a big bow at the nape of her neck.

"Mimi, please may we have some powder? Just a tiny bit, on our noses?" said Naomi.

Mimi smiled, and dabbed her scented powder-puff over the five faces.

"Let's smell us," said Shoshie, sniffing at Dvora. Dvora sniffed back at her sister.

"Lovely," she breathed, "we all smell lovely."

"When we've all finished smelling each other," said Mimi, "we should go. Monsieur Gustave will not be pleased if we're late."

"Go where?" said Dvora.

"To see a man who is going to take a photograph of us," said Rifka. "Like the Gluckmann girls, do you remember?"

"A picture of us?" asked Dvora. "Will we be able to see ourselves like that, on a card?"

"Yes," said Chava, "but only if we hurry."

"How will they do it? Does it hurt?" Dvora wanted to know.

"No, of course not. You just stand still. No one even touches you. It's all over very quickly."

"I'm scared. Don't want it," muttered Shoshie, not at all clear about what was going on around her.

"Nonsense," said Chava. "Come, I'll carry you down the stairs, and hold your hand all the way there."

"Exquisite!" cried Monsieur Gustave, clasping his hands together and sighing. "Like a bunch of fresh, new roses! One lovelier than the next!"

72

"I expect he said just the same things to the Gluckmann girls," whispered Chava to Naomi, who, Chava could see, was in danger of believing every word. "Like a doctor, to stop you feeling nervous."

"I'm not nervous," said Naomi. "It's just so exciting."

Rifka was looking at Mimi, who seemed to be deep in conversation with Madame Gustave. "I hope it's all worth it," she said.

"Of course it will be," said Chava. "Don't worry."

"Now, my beauties," said Monsieur Gustave, "come over here where we can arrange you in the most artistic way possible. Here is the backdrop I have chosen for you. Do you like it? Romantic, I think, misty and dreamy, just right. We don't want anything too brash or vulgar. Now here," he pushed a cane table across the floor, and dusted it briefly with a rather grubby rag, "is a table on which we will place an ornamental pedestal, for balance and harmony, you understand." He picked up an ugly, square stone pillar, about a foot high, and put it on the table. This, too, he dusted, and Naomi noticed that the dirty rag came away even dirtier than it was before. "Here, on the left, we will have a screen. Cane, like the table, and quite my favourite piece in the whole studio. And now, come little girls," (Rifka, Chava and Naomi frowned in annoyance) "and let me arrange you. You, Miss Rifka, is it not?, you are the tallest, and must stand at the back. Miss Chava and Miss Naomi, isn't it, in front of you, and then the babies in front of them." Monsieur Gustave's small, wrinkled hands pushed them into position. He stood back a little and looked at them. "Good. Very good. Now, the little ones, I think, should hold hands. That's right."

Dvora and Shoshanna held hands. Shoshie looked bewildered. Who was this funny man, and why was he pushing them all into a little space? What was he saying? Why did he wear a hat like a floppy saucer? Where was Mimi? Why were they having to stand so still? Now the funny man was laying a fluffy, white carpet on the floor, and telling her and Dvora to stand on it. Then he disappeared into another room and came back with some flowers and branches. The flowers were made of paper. They smelled of nothing, not like proper flowers. Chava had a branch with little, spiky leaves on it. Poor Rifka did not get a flower, because Naomi's head would hide it in the picture.

"Now hold them thus," said Monsieur Gustave, "and don't move for a moment while I look at you."

Chava remembered Ruth Gluckmann, and let her olive branch fall from her fingers until it touched the floor. She put her head to one side, and concentrated on looking elegant. Rifka was worried in case Naomi's head would hide the jet buttons on her pocket. Naomi was staring over Monsieur Gustave's shoulder at the box on legs that was soon going to perform some magic, and then there they would be forever, stuck on a piece of card, exactly as they were now. I shall grow up, she thought, and change, and get bigger, and go to America, but a bit of me will always stay just the same, printed on paper, behind glass in a frame. Dvora was looking at Mimi and a skinny lady in black talking in the corner. Her paper flower was mauve, like her ribbon. I'm hungry, she thought, and I want to go back to Mimi's house. This place is dirty. It smells of dust and glue. I wish I could always have my hair like this, but it's hot now. In winter it would be nice.

"That's perfect," squeaked Monsieur Gustave. "Don't move please, that's absolutely perfect." He ran to the camera, while the sisters stood quite still, just as he had placed them. His head disappeared under a black cloth. Would he ever come out, Shoshie wondered, and stared at the strange box for a long time without blinking. But yes, there he was, coming out again.

"Wonderful, wonderful! What subjects! What a good little girl this little girl is," he said, tickling Shoshie under the chin. "Didn't move once. She deserves a chocolate for that. You all deserve a chocolate. Mathilde! Bring the chocolate."

His wife hurried towards the girls, and offered them chocolate from a big box with a picture of a lady in furs on the lid.

"The photograph will only be ready in three weeks or so, I'm afraid," said Monsieur Gustave, "because I'm so dreadfully busy. But you will have a dozen copies just after New Year in September, and it will be a work of art, I assure you."

"Wasn't it fun?" said Chava to Naomi.

"Yes, but I felt silly standing so still. It's strange being able to talk and move and smile again."

"I want another chocolate," said Dvora. "I'm hungry."

"Ssh, don't dare ask for more," Rifka whispered angrily. "We'll be back at Mimi's soon, and you'll have all the food you can eat."

Monsieur Gustave beamed at them from the door. "Come again, little roses, come again."

"Again!" Chava laughed. "He was lucky to get us this time. If Mother knew, she'd never get over it."

"She'll know soon enough," said Rifka, "and I hope she forgives us when she sees the picture, that's all."

"I'm hungry," said Dvora.

"So let's go home," said Mimi. "What are we waiting for?"

"One for Mother, one for Mimi, one for Aunt Zehava, one for us, of course." Naomi paused. She was sitting cross-legged on her bed, watching Rifka hanging her new blue dress in the wardrobe. "Do you want to give one to David? Because that makes five, so we still have a lot left."

"No," said Rifka, "I don't think so. Not yet. I hardly know him."

"But what if he asks for one? When he comes here and sees it?"

"I'll worry about that later. He's not coming so soon, anyway."

"How do you know?" asked Chava.

"I thought you were supposed to be reading," Rifka said crossly. "I don't know, I just think, that's all. I've really no idea when he'll come. When he comes, he comes and that's that." She sat down on her bed and began to brush her hair.

"I'd like to send one to Isaac," said Naomi. "If he saw a picture of all of us, don't you think that would make him write? It would remind him of us."

"He shouldn't need reminding of his own sisters," said Chava.

"I didn't mean reminding of us like that. Just of what we all look like. Sometimes I forget what his face is like, and it makes me scared. I shut my eyes and I can't see him. I wish we had a picture of him, and I do think we should send him one of ours."

"Brilliant!" said Chava. "Really brilliant! We have, of course, his address written down, and we know just where to send the photograph. Sometimes, you know, Naomi, I wonder about you."

Naomi looked defeated. She said almost to herself: "I forgot. I forgot about needing the address. Oh, Rifka, what shall we do? How can we find him?"

Rifka sat still for a moment before she answered.

"It may be possible, but I don't know. It's only an idea."

"What? Tell us. What idea?" Naomi's face shone with hope.

"Well, the Rabbi's brother lives in New York."

"But he doesn't even know Isaac," said Chava. "He's not going to look for him in all those crowds."

"He might. I'll find out his address from the Rabbi, and I'll write to him and tell him it would be an act of charity. You're supposed to perform acts of charity. I'll do it, you'll see. I'll wait for the Rabbi tomorrow. I'm sure Isaac will write as soon as he gets the photograph. And our letters. We must all write, even the little ones, and then the Rabbi's brother will have a whole bundle of let-ters to give to Isaac when he finds him."

"Shoshie can't write," said Chava, "and Dvora can only manage things like 'dog' and 'cat' and her name."

"We'll ask them to tell us what they want to write, and we'll write it for them," said Rifka.

"I suppose it might work," said Chava grudgingly. "And if we did have a letter from Isaac, Mother would be so pleased, she might even pay our half of the money."

"Don't say a word to her about it," said Rifka. "The photo-graph will be ready in three weeks, and we'll write as soon as we get it."

Later, when her sisters were asleep, Chava lay awake a long time. So little chance of our letters and the photograph reaching Isaac, she thought. It's like throwing a bottle into the sea.

The next day, Rifka waited for the Rabbi. She sat on the low wall outside the synagogue, knowing that he was always early for the evening service. Soon she saw him, shuffling slowly down the road in his long, black coat and fur hat.

"A fur hat in this heat!" she thought, watching him as he came towards her, keeping in the shade as much as possible. She jumped off the wall and ran to greet him.

"Good evening, Rabbi."

"Rifka Bernstein, good evening to you. You are out of breath, I see. Are you bringing an important message?"

"No, I'm afraid not. I ran because I was eager to see you."

"Is there a problem? Your mother, your sisters, is someone in trouble?"

"No, it's nothing like that, Rabbi. I'm sorry to bother you before the service, but I would like you to give me your brother's address in New York."

77

"Are you going to write to my brother? I did not realize that you knew him. Didn't he leave before you were born? Or was it later? Who knows?"

Walking towards the synagogue, slowing her steps to keep pace with the old man, Rifka told him everything: about Isaac not writing, and her mother being forced to tell a lie, about the photograph and the plan they had made to surprise their mother, and to send a copy to Isaac in the hope that seeing his sisters there before his eyes would spur him to write to them. The Rabbi's brother was the only person they knew of in New York, and they thought that perhaps he could find Isaac and deliver their letters. "If," said Rifka finally, "he is as kind as you are."

The Rabbi chuckled. "Flatterer! But it is a good idea. Kind, I don't know about, but my brother is the sort of person who prides himself on knowing everyone. If anyone will find Isaac for you, he will. Come, I will write the address on that sheet of paper you are clutching so hard."

Rifka unfolded the paper and the Rabbi spread it out on the bumpy surface of the wall, and wrote on it with the pencil Rifka gave him. Then he folded the paper up, and handed it to Rifka, who put it carefully into her pocket.

"Thank you so much, Rabbi. And please say nothing of this to anyone."

"To your mother, you mean? Never fear, my silence will be like the silence of these ancient stones. Go in peace, Rifka." The old man waved his hand to her as he made his way into the synagogue.

PART TWO

Chapter VI

Mimi was leaning out of the window, waving a small, brown package above her head, and shouting to the girls in the street below:

"Hurry! For goodness sake, run, all of you! They're here! The photographs have come. Monsieur Gustave brought them himself. Oh, do hurry. I've been simply fainting with curiosity. Please, please, come along quickly!"

Rifka picked Shoshie up, and ran into the building and up the stairs. Chava and Naomi took Dvora's hands and swung her along between them. They arrived out of breath at Mimi's door, and found her waiting.

"Come in, come in. Oh, I'm sorry to make you run so, and get you out of breath, and red in the face. Just look at you all, a bunch of beetroots! But I was so excited. I can't wait to see it."

"Why," said Rifka, still panting, "didn't you open it yourself? We wouldn't have minded."

"Oh no, I would never do that. It's your picture, and you must be the first to open the package. Rifka, I think you should do it, as you're the eldest."

"No, please not. Let someone else do it. I'm a bit frightened of seeing myself all at once, like that. Let Chava do it."

"Give me the package," said Chava, and took it from Mimi's fluttering fingers. "Now everyone must sit down and calm down, and I'll take the photograph out and hold it up so that you can all see it. Then we'll look at it more closely."

"Yes," said Mimi, "that's the best way. Come, Dvora and Shoshie, sit by me, and Naomi here, and Rifka here, and Chava will soon be ready."

Everyone squeezed on to the tiny sofa and waited. Was Chava being deliberately slow and careful, thought Rifka, or was it simply that she herself was in such a hurry to see, to see at last what she had so often tried to picture in the three weeks since their visit to Monsieur Gustave's studio.

"There." Chava held the photograph up. "There we are, and aren't we all lovely?"

The girls jumped up from the sofa squealing, and ran to Chava to look more closely.

"Wait," she said, "don't all leap and shout at me. Sit down and pass it round properly."

The photograph passed from hand to hand. Shoshie pointed to herself and asked: "Who is this girl like me?" and the others laughed.

"It *is* you," said Rifka. "That's you in the picture."

"But I'm here," said Shoshie, "so I'm not in the picture. So who is it who looks like me?"

Dvora tried to explain to her little sister, but Chava said: "I know exactly what Shoshie means. It's difficult to imagine that these girls, all quiet and standing beside the lacy screen like so many dolls, are us. So much of us isn't there, and yet that's how we look, and everyone will say how exactly like us it is. But Rifka looks quite stern, and you're not a bit stern really, are you, Rifka? And Dvora, well, where are her dimples, and her funny little wrinkled nose. And Shoshie looks as if she's seen a ghost. Naomi looks dreamy and poetic, when we all know she was probably thinking about something quite boring, and ordinary, like what she had for breakfast."

82

"And you, dear Chava," said Rifka "look as if you're pretending to be some great tragic actress, all droopy and elegant."

"I was pretending something like that, as a matter of fact," said Chava placidly, "so I'm glad that's what I look like."

"Mimi," said Naomi, "you haven't said a word. What do you think of it?"

Mimi clasped the photograph to her bosom and looked solemnly at her nieces.

"I think it's beautiful. I'm overwhelmed, quite overwhelmed. I have no words. I think it's wonderful, and I can't understand all of you being so . . . so . . . I can't think of the right word, not rude exactly, but, well, everyday and matter-of-fact about it. Wait, that's all. Just wait till you're my age, and then you'll see how lovely you all were when you were young. I shall simply treasure my picture."

Mimi stood up.

"And now, we must find the frame. Your mother, my dears, will be speechless, quite, quite speechless. Come, it must be somewhere in my bedroom. We'll find it if we have to look all morning."

The photograph was put away carefully, and the girls followed Mimi out of the room.

"You must forgive the mess, my darlings," she said as they went into the bedroom. "I was still in bed when Shmuel—I mean Gustave—arrived with the package. For anything else, I can tell you, I wouldn't have left my bed at such an unearthly hour. He came at nine o'clock. And since he left, I've been in such a fever of excitement that I haven't dressed, or tidied the room, or eaten or anything. You should have seen me! You would have laughed. Pacing up and down, picking the package up, putting it back, going to the window. I felt just like a child."

She flung the embroidered silk counterpane over the unmade

83

bed and said: "There, now, all of you sit down while I try and think where that frame is. I should have thought of it sooner really."

"I'll help you look," said Dvora. "I'm good at finding things. What is the frame like?"

"Well, it's square, a little bigger than the photograph as I remember, and it's made out of dark green velvet, padded. If there's another photograph in it, we'll just take it out and put yours in."

Dvora was given one drawer to look through, and Mimi started flinging clothes out of another. Rifka was·told to go through the shoe-boxes at the bottom of the wardrobe, and Chava looked in the hat-boxes among the toques and the picture-hats, with their veils·and satin-ribbons, and artificial flowers, because as Mimi said: "You just never know with me, I might have put it anywhere." Naomi sat at the tiny writing desk by the window and went through the two little drawers and the four cubby holes, turning over bundles of letters, some tied with blue ribbons, and some with string, others pushed into larger envelopes and not tied up at all. Love letters, thought Naomi, I'm sure that's what they are. The best ones tied in ribbons, the next best in string, and the boring ones just pushed together in a pile, and stuck into an envelope. One cubby hole of the desk, Naomi knew, was full of old photographs, mostly of Mimi and her beaux. The girls had often looked at them, marvelling at the clothes, and the strange buildings in faraway cities that they could see sometimes in the background. Perhaps there's a picture here of Max, thought Naomi. He'll be coming soon. He said September, and it's been September for a week already. Maybe one day our nieces will come across the picture of us in a drawer, and think how old-fashioned our clothes are, and how funny we look. It makes me feel peculiar to think about it.

"Is this it, Mimi?" Dvora held up a velvet, padded frame which

84

she had found lying between two pairs of mauve kid gloves.

"Yes, yes, you clever little thing," said Mimi. "Of course that's it, and look, all of you, isn't it perfect? Now run, one of you, and get the picture, while I remove this old thing that's in here . . ." Mimi took the frame from Dvora and stopped talking suddenly.

"What's the matter, Mimi? What's wrong?" said Chava.

"Wrong? What should be wrong? Nothing, nothing. I was just remembering the photograph that's here. Look, girls, guess who it is? It's Max. Max who will be here soon, although it's strange he's sent me no word. Perhaps he won't come after all."

"Let me see," said Chava.

"And me," said Naomi.

"You can all see. There." Mimi gave the frame to Rifka and the others crowded around her.

"He's so handsome, Mimi," said Naomi. "Like a prince. Look how tall he is! You only reach his shoulder."

"I like his uniform," said Chava. "And did you ever see such shiny boots?"

"When is he coming?" Dvora wanted to know.

"Soon, darling, I hope," said Mimi. "But he won't look like this. This was long ago when we were both very young."

"But you still look a bit like you in that picture," said Dvora, "so why won't he?"

"It's kind of you to say so, Dvora, but you know I have to work very hard to look even a bit like I used to. Look at me now, before I've done all that hard work with hairbrushes and pins, and rouges and corsets and pretty dresses. I look like what I am, an elderly lady. Now go, Chava, or somebody, and fetch your picture, while I remove poor Max from here and put him in some box or other. Now let me see . . ." Mimi picked up a pair of scissors and eased open the little silver clasps that held the back of the frame in place. She slid the photograph of Max out from under the glass.

85

"I'll just put him here among the scarves for the moment," she began, but Naomi said:

"No, Mimi, give the picture to me, and I'll put it here in the desk with the others. That's the right place for it."

"'Out of the mouths of babes and sucklings, cometh forth wisdom'" said Mimi. "Naomi, you're quite right. Here, put him in with the others, and let's see how you all look in this pretty frame." She pushed the picture into position, and replaced the silver clasps at the back. "There, now, won't your mother be overjoyed when she sees that?"

"It's really lovely, Mimi," said Rifka. "Thank you so much. You are kind. As soon as I start working I'll save the money to pay you back."

"Oh, my goodness!" Mimi put her hand to her mouth. "I completely forgot to tell you. There's nothing to pay. That's why Shmuel, Gustave, I mean, came here with the package, to tell me *that*, instead of us going to the studio to pay when we collected the photographs. He's managed to fix his account books somehow, so that that ghastly wife of his won't ask questions, but he didn't want her reminded of our existence by a visit. Isn't that marvellous?"

"But why, Mimi?" asked Chava. "Why should he do that for us?"

Mimi smiled. "For me, you mean. I told you, he used to love me madly. Didn't I tell you? Didn't you believe me? He has, he said, fond memories of me. Those were his very words: 'fond memories'."

"Well," said Chava, "that's really splendid, but we'll tell Mother that you paid, Mimi, if she asks us. Will you mind that?"

"Not in the least. Let her think I'm rich and generous. It might make her feel more kindly towards me."

"I'll tell her to invite you to the house on her birthday," said Rifka quietly. "I shall insist upon it. She will, you'll see, Mimi. I

86

want you to be there when she opens her present."

"I wish we didn't have to wait till Saturday," said Naomi. "I'd like to give it to her now."

"No, we'll wait," said Rifka "and we'll have to explain very carefully to the little ones that the photograph is an absolute secret."

"You don't need to explain to me," said Dvora with great dignity. "I understand about secrets, and you don't have to worry about Shoshie because I'll explain to her."

"Thank you, Dvora," said Rifka, trying not to smile, "that will be a very great help to us, and make it a lovely surprise for Mother."

"Now, children, come," said Mimi. "I'm so hungry from all the excitement, I could eat for a week. Let's go and see what there is in the house."

"That's better," said Mimi a little later, having finished her breakfast of cold, stuffed cabbage from the day before, grapes, and a handful of fresh dates. "If there were anything else to eat, I could eat it, but there's nothing left now except sweets and titbits, so I'll just nibble a little from time to time as we talk. Tell me your news, all of you. I haven't seen you since New Year, and now it's nearly Yom Kippur already, and I expect there's a great deal of news I don't know about."

"Not very much," said Rifka, "nothing much has happened at all. Mother won't let me fast again this year. She says God allows children to eat, even on Yom Kippur, but I'm thirteen, after all."

"Count yourself lucky," said Mimi. "The Fast becomes more difficult every year."

"Why do you do it, Mimi?" said Chava. "I've never understood. You never go to the synagogue, you don't keep Kosher, so what's the point of fasting?"

87

"I really don't know, Chava, and I ask myself every year. Habit, tradition, trying to make up to God for being so slapdash the rest of the year—I don't understand it myself. But I do it. Every year. It makes me feel just the way I did when I was young, like a very good girl for a whole day."

"That's the reason, then," Chava laughed. "You like feeling like a good girl from time to time."

"And," said Mimi, "you can't imagine how blissful food tastes when the Fast is over. Every mouthful is a treat. But enough talking about food. Tell me, Rifka, how is your young man? Has he been to the house?"

Rifka looked at her hands. "Yes, he came. With Mrs. Levinsky. Mother was quite flustered, but he spent most of his time feeding the rabbits with the little ones. Menahem, luckily, was visiting his grandmother."

"David is lovely," said Shoshie.

"He loves animals," explained Dvora. "The cat followed him right up the stairs and into our house."

". . . and Mother chased it away with a broom because she said it brought fleas," put in Naomi.

"And I cried," said Shoshie. "I wanted to give it milk."

"Will you ever bring this young man to see me?" said Mimi. "Aren't I going to be allowed to have a peep at him? I'll tell you, Rifka, never fear, if he's the right one for you."

"He's going to Europe in April," said Chava. "To study agriculture in Germany, I think. For two years."

"Oh, no!" said Mimi, "how dreadful! Poor Rifka! Won't you miss him? When did you hear this?"

"Just the other week," said Rifka, "and I don't know if I'll miss him or not. I don't really know him very well yet."

"But you like him, don't you?" Mimi wanted to know. "You told me you did."

"Yes, I do." Rifka fell silent. Of course I'll miss him, she thought. But I won't let anyone see. And he'll write to me. He said he would. I shall have letters just for me to read and no one else. "But," she added, as she noticed the others looking at her, "he will know a lot about farming and fruit-growing when he comes back. He wants to be a farmer."

"Well," said Mimi, "if you still want to marry him knowing that, then your love must be very great indeed. Up early feeding chickens and I don't know what, never going to parties or wearing nice clothes, never seeing anyone,—no, I could never do it." Mimi shuddered.

"I won't mind, I don't think," said Rifka. "It'll be nicer than working in the shop."

"She starts in the Gluckmann shop next week," said Chava. "And we all have to go back to school and dreadful Mr. Lemel with his long ruler for poking naughty children in the side with," said Naomi.

"And his silly, chanting rules." Chava put on a voice that was squeaky and deep at the same time:

"Repeat after me, children: 'Remember while you drink and eat, that parallel lines don't ever meet.' I'd much rather work with lots of lovely cakes."

"So would I," said Naomi. "He never likes anything we do. I wrote a poem just before the summer, and he said it was childish and sentimental."

"Well, it was," said Chava.

"It wasn't." Mimi saw that Naomi was close to tears and put in swiftly: "Even if it was, Naomi, it's nothing to be ashamed of. You are a child, after all, so what does he want from you? And there's nothing wrong with sentimental poems. If I can't weep a little over a poem, then I'm really disappointed. I'm sure your poem is beautiful, Naomi. Can you remember it, to say to me?"

"No, not really," said Naomi.

"Yes, she can," said Chava at the same moment. "She's being modest. She knows all her own poems by heart. Go on, Naomi. It wasn't so bad, for a poem."

Naomi hesitated. "Oh, well," she said, "if you all want me to. Are you sure? It's quite long."

"Yes, we're sure," said Mimi. "Pray silence, everyone for a recitation by Mademoiselle Naomi Bernstein."

Naomi coughed and began to speak:

> "The wings of the dove are white,
> The leaves on the trees are new,
> The king has sent his youngest son
> Over the sea of blue.
>
> He met a lady fair
> In a green and distant land,
> And he asked the lovely maiden
> If he could hold her hand.
>
> She let him bring her rubies
> And bring her rings of gold,
> And he said that he would love her
> Until they both were old
>
> But the prince sailed home one morning
> And the lady waited long,
> And when he never came again
> She sang a sad, sad song.
>
> She walked all day in the garden
> Crying bitter tears,
> And her heart was heavy and broken
> For years and years and years."

"Bravo!" shouted Mimi when Naomi had finished. "Lovely! What a clever child you are! It's gloriously sad, just like a poem should be."

"I suppose it's not bad considering you're only eight," said Chava, "but Mr. Lemel's right. It is sentimental."

"I think it's beautiful," said Rifka, almost angrily. "I really do."

"Love," said Mimi, "that's what it is. You're in love, Rifka. I can tell. It makes you very soft on the inside. You cry at the least little thing, isn't that so?"

"Nonsense, Mimi, of course I don't," said Rifka, marvelling inwardly at how clever Mimi was at knowing such things. Rifka had felt like weeping quite often recently over all sorts of silly things: sunsets, and Shoshie sleeping, and some of Mother's old songs, and now, over Naomi's poem. But in love? The words seemed much too grown-up for what she was feeling.

"Have a sugared almond, anyway," said Mimi. "Sweets are very comforting when you're in love, and they're also nice when you aren't, so you may each have one, for making it such a lovely morning. Haven't we had fun? The picture, the frame, Naomi's poem: it's been like a party."

"Want a pink one," said Shoshie.

"There you are, little flower, there's a pink one for you," said Mimi. "You know I always save them especially." She stood up. "Now if you'll wait here, I'll go and put on some clothes and arrange my face and hair a little, and then we can all go down to the market and buy lots of lovely things." Just as she turned to go into the bedroom, someone knocked at the door.

"Rifka, go and see who that is, please, will you? I'm not expecting anyone, but if it's someone interesting, ask them to wait with you." Mimi disappeared into the bedroom and shut the door. Rifka went to the front door and opened it. An old man stood there, thin and upright, with a white moustache carefully waxed into two jaunty points. His faded blue eyes twinkled beneath bushy, white eyebrows. A gold chain hung across his waistcoat and disappeared into the breast pocket of a smart grey suit. Rifka noticed that his shoes were shiny even after having walked through the dusty streets, and that there was a gold signet ring on one of the fingers of the well-manicured hand holding a brand-new straw hat.

"Excuse me," he said in what Rifka at first thought was very bad Yiddish, and later realized was very good German. "Does Miss Miriam Bernstein live here?"

"Yes, she does," said Rifka. "Miss Miriam Bernstein is my aunt. Please come in and sit down, and she will be with us in a moment."

"Thank you, my dear. I should like to sit down, I should indeed. A great many stairs to climb to this flat, is that not so?"

"Yes, it is," said Rifka. "Please come and wait in here. These are my sisters."

"Enchanted, my dears," said the old man. "And now let me present myself to all you pretty young ladies. I am Maximilian von Eschenloer."

"Mimi's Max!" said Chava in a loud, astonished voice before she could stop herself.

"Exactly!" said the old gentleman, smiling under his moustaches. "Mimi's Max."

"And then," said Naomi, "Mimi came out in a lovely dress with frills coloured like the sky when it's very pale, and she was looking pink and shy, and she just stood there and couldn't say a word. She kept smiling at Max, and opening her mouth and closing it again."

"Surely she said something in the end, didn't she?" said Sarah, snipping the brown wool with which she was darning stockings for the winter. "She can't have stood there for more than a few minutes."

"It was more like a few seconds, really," said Chava. "Naomi is exaggerating, as usual."

"I'm not. It was ages. I'm sure Mimi and Max must have felt it was ages."

"Girls, please, don't start quarelling now," said Sarah. "I'm anxious to hear what happened, but squeezing the story out of you is like wringing water from dry clothes. Did they embrace?"

"Yes," said Rifka, "but very politely. A kiss on each cheek, like two old ladies meeting in the street. Then Mimi started talking about making coffee."

"But I could see," added Chava, "that she wasn't in any mood for making coffee. She would have put out salt instead of sugar."

". . . so Chava and I made it. And we had Turkish Delight and sugared almonds with it, because there was no cake."

"Enough, enough! I can't bear it," said Sarah. "I want to hear about Mimi and Max, and all you can tell me about is cups of coffee. Will no-one tell me what happened?"

Rifka, Chava and Naomi looked at one another. Then Naomi said: "Nothing really did happen."

"What do you mean, nothing happened?" said Sarah, looking at that moment as crestfallen as Dvora did when Naomi's stories were not progressing as she wanted them to.

"She means, Mother," said Rifka patiently, "that nothing happened. We all sat about drinking coffee, and Mimi and Max were talking about dances and parties and operas they had been to together."

"And Max was telling us about the lady who owns the pension where he's staying. He said she looked like a stick of asparagus: thin and greenish," said Chava. "And then we all went to the market to buy food."

"Max as well?" Sarah asked.

"Yes, Max as well. Everyone in the market treated Max and Mimi like a king and queen." Rifka laughed as she remembered the scene. "Mimi introduced Max so formally to all her favourite stallholders. She even made him a Count for the occasion! 'This is my friend, Count Maximilian von Eschenloer, from Strasbourg,' she said, and Max bowed from the waist, and the stallholders looked overawed and pressed extra fruit and vegetables into our baskets."

"And then what?" said Sarah.

"Nothing," said Chava. "We helped them take the food up, and then we came home."

"And I've waited all afternoon to hear all about it, and we put the little ones to bed early, and now I see it was hardly worth it. Nothing seems to have happened, just as you said."

"What did you expect, Mother, really?" said Chava.

"I don't know. Something more dramatic, knowing Mimi."

"Maybe he should have ridden off into the hills with her on the back of a white charger," Chava laughed.

"Yes, something like that," said Sarah, and then she laughed too. "Oh, Chavale, you're teasing me! Of course I wasn't expecting that, exactly, but I did hope . . ."

"He's an old man, Mother," said Rifka, "don't forget that."

"Yes, that's true," said Sarah. "Well, I shall have to have a look at him myself, that's all. We'll invite them here one day. Perhaps morning coffee will be the best." She put aside the darned stocking, and took up another. Rifka looked at her sisters. Chava nodded quickly, and Naomi blushed. Rifka took a deep breath and said:

"I think you should invite them on your birthday. It's also the Sabbath, so it's very suitable, and I'm sure they won't be busy."

"Rifka, don't tell me you've forgotten!" Sarah looked shocked. "Mr. and Mrs. Levinsky and David are coming then."

"I haven't forgotten at all. Mimi would like to meet them. She told me so."

"Well, I don't think they should all come together . . ." Sarah began.

"Why not?" asked Chava.

"Because," Sarah threaded a needle, thinking of how to answer. "It's too many people, too much work."

"Oh, Mother, when was any work too much for you? You're ashamed to say it, that's all." Chava sounded angry.

"Ashamed to say what?"

"That you're afraid that Mrs. Levinsky will think Mimi is some-how too talkative, or funnily dressed, or not quite good enough for her. Say it. You know it's true."

"It's not true!" Sarah sounded indignant.

"Then invite them. Where's the harm?"

Sarah sighed. "I suppose I shall have to, or you will think . . . what you think."

"Then can we tell Mimi?" Rifka was smiling.

"Tell her, tell her, but also please tell her to invite Max. At least I shall see him. What, I wonder, will they do with themselves while he's in Jerusalem?"

"Mimi is going to show him all the places that are in the Bible of his religion," said Naomi. "And they will travel to Tiberias, which Max says is a very important place because of the Sea of Galilee."

"If only he were not a Christian," said Sarah, "Mimi might marry him and settle down to a more ordinary sort of life."

"I don't think Mimi cares about his religion at all," said Chava.

"I'm sure you're right," Sarah replied, "and it's one of the things I can't understand about your aunt. How a brother and sister can be so different, I'll never understand. Your beloved father was so devout."

The girls did not answer. For a while they sat around the table in silence, and the lamp at Sarah's elbow enclosed them in a circle of soft, yellow light that left the corners of the room in darkness, and stretched their shadows into strange shapes on the wall.

"Such a funny thing happened while you were out," Sarah's voice broke into the stillness that had fallen. The girls looked up. "The Old Man came. Here. He's never been before. I've hardly ever spoken to him. When I saw him coming up the stairs, so frail and weak and old, I wanted to shout to him that no, no, I would come down. But then I thought he might be offended. So I let him come. I sat him down there, in your chair, Rifka, and it was ten minutes before he found his breath again and was able to speak. Such wheezing and sighing and coughing! I offered him tea, of course, but he said he never eats or drinks out of his own house, because he can never be sure."

"Sure of what?" asked Naomi.

"Sure that I keep a really Kosher kitchen. I think maybe, many years ago, he was a rabbi. Certainly he's the most devout and God-loving man that I know."

"Why did he come?" Chava asked.

"I'm coming to that. It was most extraordinary. He asked me if I would allow Dvora and Shoshanna to visit him again. I said, of course, and I thought to myself: poor old man, perhaps they remind him of grandchildren he never had. Or grandchildren he once had, and has now lost, which would be even worse. I hinted at something of the sort, and he was quite sharp with me, and said no, it was because they had taken such an interest, and because Dvora had asked such intelligent questions. So I thanked him and told him I'll send them down tomorrow afternoon, and he nodded, and said goodbye, and then I helped him downstairs to his rooms. I took him right inside. There's nothing in there but books. A bed, a table and two chairs, and books, books, books, piled wherever you can think of. No cushions, no food, no pictures, nothing comfortable and soft, only old books with tiny letters. Is it any wonder the Old Man can hardly see?"

"The soft and comfortable things for him are probably in the books," said Naomi, "so he doesn't need them in the furniture."

"You can say what you like," said Sarah, "but I know that whatever wisdom is in a book to make a man learned and happy, it can never take the place of a soft pillow under his head, or a warm blanket for the winter. And talking of warm blankets, although it's a long time till we need them, reminds me that you should all be in your beds."

The girls kissed Sarah goodnight, and went into the kitchen to wash. Then they walked along the dark balcony to their room, on tiptoe, so as not to wake Dvora and Shoshie.

Rifka was dreaming of a small cloud dropping rain on her cheek. It was soft and very wet. She could feel the softness and the wetness. Then the cloud turned into a tiny kitten, clawing at her arm. The kitten was meowing, sad, sad noise like crying, like a child crying, like Shoshie crying when she was a baby. Immediately, Rifka sprang up, wide awake.

"Rifka, oh Rifka," said Shoshie's voice, bubbling with tears.

"Shoshie, is that you? Darling little one, what is it, why are you crying?"

"I saw horrible things." Rifka managed to make out the words through the weeping.

"You had a dream, Shoshie, that's all it was. It wasn't real. Dreams are never real. Come, dry your eyes, and blow your nose, and jump into bed with me."

A little later, with Shoshie lying in the curve of her arm, Rifka said: "Do you want to tell me about your horrid dream? If you talk about it, sometimes it doesn't seem so bad."

"The cat. The rabbits ran away from the cage. The cat scratched them. Then the rabbits died. Then Menahem came. He was shouting. But he was big."

"Grown-up?"

"No, big like a giant. He had big shoes. He could tread on us."

"Well, Menahem's a silly, skinny little boy, not much bigger than you. He'll even be quite little when he's grown-up."

"Really? Not a giant?"

"No, never. I promise you. Now, you lie there and close your eyes, and I'll tell you lovely things to think about, and then you'll dream about them when you're asleep."

"Can I stay with you?"

"Yes," said Rifka, "you can stay." She began in a soft voice to tell Shoshie about all the loveliest things she could think of: butterflies and flowers and rainbows and fluffy clouds and puppies and dolls in silk dresses, and soon, before she had finished her list, Shoshie was asleep. Rifka pulled her arm out from under her little sister's neck, gently so as not to disturb her, and settled back on her pillow, pleasantly aware of the warm little body at her side. Shoshie was lying just as she used to lie when she was a baby, with one fist curled under her cheek and her mouth a little open. It's a long time, thought Rifka, since she's woken up like this. When she was tiny, I had her next to me almost every night, so that she wouldn't wake the whole house. Of course, it's good that she's growing up and sleeping so well, but oh, how lovely it is to cuddle up together again. She smells so sweet. It's not fair that such a little thing should have bad dreams, but I'm glad, so glad that she had one tonight.

Chapter VII

. . . and I know that what we have asked you to do is a very hard thing. There must be quite a lot of people there, where you are, but our Rabbi, your brother, says you are good at finding people. When you find Isaac, please will you give him the photograph and all our letters. Thank you very much. We will wait for your answer every day, so I hope it comes quite soon. Happy New Year, even if it is a little late,

from Rifka Bernstein

From Rifka's letter to Isaac

. . . Mother's birthday was on Saturday, and even though we always do something a little special on her birthday, this year it was so grand that it almost turned out to be a party. We had a lot of people in the afternoon. Mimi and her old beau, who is called Maximilian von Eschenloer, (but we call him Max) and Mr. and Mrs. Levinsky and their son David, who is going to be my husband when I'm sixteen, I think. At least, that is what the mothers are trying to arrange. He is very nice, but I don't know yet if he is nice enough to be with forever. Sometimes I think maybe no-one is as nice as that, and you should just take the best you can

99

get. Mimi says, if it's the right person, you know at once, but I don't think it's as easy as that. I think it's confusing, love, and most of the time you don't know what's going on inside you at all, and you feel strange. But I like him. Anyway, they were there, and Mother was very shy and pink when Mrs. Levinsky gave her a present: a silk shawl, embroidered with huge scarlet flowers, like poppies, only with more petals. Mother said how lovely it was, but I know she will never wear it, except perhaps to the Levinsky's house, so as not to be rude. Can you see Mother in scarlet poppies? That's the kind of person Mrs. Levinsky is—she gives presents that she would like to get, without really thinking what the other person would like. Then the shawl was passed around (and Mimi made everyone laugh, even Mother, when she put it round her shoulders, and took a marigold from the vase and held it between her teeth and pretended to be a Spanish dancer. Drumming her heels on the floor, with her hands thrown up above her head—can you imagine it?).

After that, we all sat round the table, and we could all see, me and Chava and Naomi, that is, that Mother was a little upset that we had given her nothing at all. Usually, as you know, we make her something like a pincushion or a picture or something. But we'd given her nothing, and you could see that she kept on wondering why, even though she couldn't say anything. Also, she was hoping, maybe, for a letter from you the day before, and so she looked a little pale at the tea-table. During all the excitement with the shawl, Chava had hidden Shoshie in the kitchen, and told her to stay there until she was called. We had put our parcel behind the bread jar, and when everyone was sitting down, Mother (at last!) noticed that Shoshie wasn't there. Chava said that she would go and fetch her, and went into the kitchen. Then she brought her in, carrying the parcel, and Shoshie went right up to Mother, and dropped it on her plate, and mumbled something. She looked so pretty. You wouldn't believe how she's grown, and she blushed till her face was as pink as her hair ribbon. Then Mother opened the parcel, and you should have seen her face! She simply didn't know what to say, just sat on her chair and started crying and laughing at the same time, and hugging the photograph as if it were a precious child. It's lucky that it was in Mimi's velvet frame, or the poor thing would have been all bent out of shape, and soaked through with tears. Then while Mimi and Max and the Levinskys exclaimed over it, Mother kissed us, and in the end she put it on the sideboard, right in the middle. She moved the fruit bowl right over to the edge, nearly, and put our picture in the most important position.

Later, when the Levinskys had gone home, we told her (because she asked us) that Mimi had paid for it all, (this isn't true, but it's too long a story to tell now) and she kissed Mimi and thanked her, and said she had never had a better present, and the two of them behaved as though there had never been a cross word between them, and soon they were gossiping as if they saw each other every week. They stayed (Mimi and Max, that is) until quite late, and Mother took out the brandy bottle, and I was allowed one sip, too, but I didn't like it very much. Dvora and Shoshie were allowed to sit up late for a treat, and they both fell asleep on the sofa, and we all forgot about them, and later on we had to carry them off to their room like plump little bundles of washing. We didn't even try to undress them, and they were astounded next morning when they woke up fully dressed, and they both rushed around making a noise and asking to be told about what had happened over and over again.

This letter is too long already, so I shall stop. We have to write in our room, so that Mother won't see. Writing to you is also partly a surprise for her. We are all saying: "Please, please write us a letter as soon as you can, so that Mother will have an even better gift than our photograph!" Here at the bottom I am going to write what Shoshie is telling me to write, so that is her letter to you.

Love, and a kiss from
Rifka

From Shoshie

Isaac, why don't you come back home? Mimi gave me a ribbon. Pink ribbon. I like feeding the rabbits. There is a cat who is an orange cat. I am three. I have two dolls, a doll called Buba and a doll called Luba. Luba is fine, but Buba's arm is broke but David can mend it.

From Chava's letter to Isaac

. . . And you should see Mimi these days. She's just like a young girl, or perhaps more like a young girl than ever. It's funny to think it's all because of Max. He's so thin and old and solemn, and he tells the most dreadful stories that go on and on for ever, and we all have to sit there looking polite, and Mimi bats her eyelashes. She really does—it's not just something the books say! During the day she carries a parasol, and in the evening she takes a fan with her wherever she goes, and waves it about. The fans are very old. They come from what we all call the dressing-up drawer. Max calls her things like "my little pigeon" and "my pretty mouse". Can you believe that? Naomi thinks it's all marvellous and romantic, and much better than Rifka and David who just gaze at each other across the room without saying anything, but if someone called me a mouse or a pigeon, I'd stick my tongue out at him. Mimi is also interested now in things she was never interested in before: old places that Max says are holy, pottery from thousands of years ago, and damp and dusty buildings. She and Max walk a lot in the Old City. We are all wondering if she will marry him, and go and live in Strasbourg. I don't think she should, and when I talk to her on my own, I shall tell her. It's difficult to find her alone while Max is here. Naomi wants a wedding. I think she wants a new dress. The poor thing always has to wear Rifka's and mine. Max says he is longing to take Mimi back with him. He describes his house (his carpets, his silver, his polished mahogany furniture) and the beautiful countryside round about, trying to tempt Mimi away. I think he thinks Jerusalem is hot and dirty as well as being holy and interesting. Mimi feels tempted, and talks a lot about the dresses she will have made for her in Europe, and the boulevards lined with chestnut trees. She says that there is not one speck of green anywhere here, and it's true that the summer has been very hot. We all feel like buns that have been baked too long. Is it hot where you are? Are there trees and avenues? I wish you would write and tell us what everything is like. We often wonder about it.

Rifka tells me that she has written all about the Presentation of the Photograph, so I don't have to tell you about that, but did she tell you how she woke us up at six o'clock in the morning on Friday to wash our hair? We couldn't do it in the afternoon as usual, because there was so much baking to be done, for the birthday, so we were all dragged out of bed at dawn, and our heads dipped in the tin bath, and soaped, and then jugs of cold water were poured all over us. Then we sat in the sun to dry it, looking like a row of wax dolls, with our heads throbbing. When Rifka washes hair, she does it thoroughly, just the way she does everything, and your scalp feels sore for hours.

All the neighbours have been to see the photograph. Mrs. Friedman came to see it specially, wiping her hands on her apron before she picked it up. Menahem was at school when she came, and he's been trying to see it too, but Dvora is being very clever and not letting him into the house unless he promises to let her and Shoshie feed and stroke the rabbits every day. The Old Man sent a message that Dvora and Shoshie should bring it for him to look at. Mimi has shown hers to all her card-playing ladies and has also taken it with her round the market. The postman said how lovely we were when Mother brought him in to show it to him, and so did the milkman. Mother has to go and see Mrs. Gluckmann, to arrange about Rifka starting work, so she will see it too, I suppose. She happened to mention when she was here with a picture of her daughters a few weeks ago, that Ruth still has a great fondness for you! Maybe one day she'll come after you to America and find you, so BEWARE! I'm now going to write down what Dvora wants to say to you, so I'll stop.

Love from

Chava

P.S. Dvora wants to write a few words herself first. She has learned them at school.

Dvora's letter to Isaac (on her own)

Dvora Bernstein. I am a girl. I live in a house. I am good.

Dvora's letter to Isaac (dictated to Chava)

Isaac, do you remember the cat? He's like our cat now, because he nearly lives in our house. He used to like the Friedmans' because of the fish scraps, but now they've stopped giving the cat fish scraps, because Menahem is frightened that the cat will eat the rabbits. I think that's stupid. The rabbits are in a cage, but Menahem is stupid. The cat came to us one day and Mother was out, and I gave him half a plate of chopped liver, so now he likes us, and I give bits of food to him all the time and then I tell Mother Shoshie has eaten the food. Mother thinks the cat is dirty, but he's not. He's clean. Cleaning himself is the best thing he does, and he can bend over backwards and reach his back right near the tail with his tongue. I can't do that. I've tried. So I know the cat is clever. Rifka says the cat is ginger, but he's all sorts of colours: brown in some places, and white and yellow in some places, all in funny stripes if you look at him in little bits. He's only orange when you see him all together in a big lump.

I go and visit the Old Man sometimes. Shoshie comes too. She is very good and not noisy because I look after her. The Old Man has books with coloured pictures. He tells us stories from the Bible. They are nice stories, but hard for Shoshie, but I make them easy for her and explain everything.

Menahem is thinking if it's alright to let us feed his rabbits. He wants to see the photograph, but I won't let him unless he says we can feed Blacky and Whitey. That is what the rabbits are called. Do you like the photograph? I think it's lovely, because I look pretty. Everyone says how pretty I look, and Rifka, Chava, Naomi and Shoshie are pretty, too, so we have a lot of people saying "How lovely!" all day long. I like that. You should send us a present from America. It will be my birthday in the spring. I will be six and soon Shoshie will be four.

Love from

Dvora

From Naomi's letter to Isaac

. . . She doesn't say much about him, but I think she thinks about him all the time. She looks different, too, like an older Rifka somehow, and doesn't smile and play around so much, but her face on the outside always looks as if she's smiling inside. Do you know what I mean? David is very nice. He's not very handsome, but he has very long fingers, and he's tall and thin. He speaks quietly, so you have to listen to everything very hard. Maybe he is shy, and speaks louder to Rifka, because he knows her better than he knows us. He has only been to the house twice, no, three times. Once on Mother's birthday, and once before that, and then yesterday again, because he promised Shoshie he would mend her doll, and he did. Rifka says he is going to be a farmer, and when they live on their farm, they'll let me feed the chickens. Then when I'm sixteen, I can come to New York and feed chickens there because I shall be very good at it by then. Are there any farms in New York? Rifka is starting work in Gluckmann's Bakery next week. Mother has been making some special work-dresses for her. Boring brown dresses, so that she'll look the same colour as the crusts on the bread, nearly. I think it would be nice to work in that shop, because it smells good and the cakes are lovely, but Rifka is a little nervous about making mistakes with money when people buy from her. Chava has been playing "shop" with her for practice. You remember how Rifka could never add up properly in her head, and always has to use her fingers? Well, she worries about that now. We say, me and Chava, that it doesn't matter, but she gets cross when we say that, and mutters: "Have you ever seen anyone in shops or in the market, adding up on their fingers?" She's right, I never have. Do they add up in their heads or on their fingers in New York? Chava says Rifka can use paper and pencil and write it all down, but that's no good because she still has to use her fingers, and anyway, she says it would take so long that the bread would be stale by the time she's finished. You can see that what she would really like to do would be to sit at home and hem sheets for when she is married.

Chava says she told you that Mimi may be getting married at last. We will miss her so much if she goes, but it all sounds so wonderful there that I'm sure she will. Max says they have a real lawn in their garden and beds of roses, and parties in the winter. He says I can come and stay with them, and eat in hotels, and go to the theatre in a carriage. Max loves Mimi so much. He holds her hand, and puts her shawl around her shoulders when it's time for them to go home, and he tells her how pretty she is all the time, and buys her little presents. I would like to marry someone like Max. He tells wonderful stories, too, about his life as a soldier, and things that he has seen on his travels. He has been to so many countries, and can tell you everything about them: which mountain is highest, and the names of the rivers and towns, and all about their history. I could listen to him forever.

I am going to write lots of poems and stories and make a book and send it to you as soon as you write and tell us your address. I'm sure you must have a good reason for not writing, like being very busy and going to different parties all the time, but Chava teases me and says you might be ill, or poor, or even dead, and although I know it's not true, I think about it at night sometimes. I can't help it, and then I have bad dreams. One night, I dreamt you were alone in the middle of a forest, and it was so full of tall trees that you couldn't move, or find your way. And the wood was full of people, only then they turned out to be only statues of people, and when you spoke to them to try and find your way home, they couldn't answer. It was horrible.

Mother says I can have a new dress when Rifka gets married, but if Mimi gets married, and I go and visit her, then I'll have one before that, so I hope she does. In the photograph, you can't see that all our ribbons are lovely colours. Mimi gave them to us as a present on the day when we went to the studio. Mine is yellow. Dvora and Shoshie have just brought Menahem in so that he can admire them in the photograph. That means he has agreed (at last!) that they can play with the rabbits. Thank goodness for that. It used to be such a struggle every day to creep over to the hutch and back without a fight. Maybe now they'll become friends. Maybe Menahem is not as bad as he looks. The little ones are making lots of friends. I went to fetch them home from the Old Man's room yesterday evening, and found all three of them asleep—Shoshie on the floor, Dvora on the bed, and the Old Man in his chair. He was snoring and so was Shoshie.

I love you, and miss you, and wait, wait, wait, for you to write and tell us all about every single thing that you have been doing.

A big hug and a kiss from your sister
Naomi

Chapter VIII

SPRING 1914

Outside, the grey February sky clamped down on the city like the inside of a saucepan lid. Rain fell from time to time, and broke into patterns on the glass panes of closed windows, running into streams, and gathering in pools, and scattering into flying drops with each fresh gust of wind. Inside her flat, Mimi was lighting the lamp.

"Not because we need it," she said, as the opalescent globe shone comfortingly yellow, "but only to make a change from grey everywhere. Outside and inside. I've yet to meet someone who can be really happy in February."

"Mimi," said Chava, "is it true, what you told us last week?"

"What did I tell you? About Max, you mean? Yes, my angel, quite true. I've decided, finally, after thinking and thinking all through the winter. Don't you find winter good for thinking?" She began to wander about the room, and stopped to pick up an ornament which she began to dust vaguely with the sleeve of her dress. "There, that's better. As soon as there's a fine day, I'm going to clean this place from top to bottom." She turned to face the girls. Dvora and Shoshie were drawing a collection of animals and flowers on old scraps of paper, but Rifka, Chava and Naomi were looking at her expectantly.

"I'm not going to marry him, and that's that," she announced. "And before you all start shouting at me, I'll tell you why."

"I'm not going to shout," said Chava. "I'm pleased. I never did think it was a good idea."

"No, I remember," said Mimi. "You told me I shouldn't when Max first came. Well, I was overwhelmed by him, and I should have known better, at my age, to let myself be carried away by gifts and kind, flattering words."

"But you told him you would," said Naomi, disappointed. "You were going to join him in April. It was all arranged. And then we could have come and visited you in his house. Don't you remember all the things he said about his house? Don't you want to live in such a grand place?"

"No, my little Naomi, I don't, and I'll tell you why. In such a home, in such a place, I wouldn't be me, I'd be someone else. I couldn't get up when I wanted, dress when I wanted, eat when I wanted, visit whoever I chose to visit, wear what I love wearing—I'd become a completely different person. I'd have to do everything Max's way because he's too old to change his habits now, and I know him, oh dear me, yes, I know him. Look at me now—you don't find anything wrong and neither do I, but a wife in a dressing gown at three o'clock in the afternoon would kill him in a year. He doesn't approve of ladies playing cards, and though he thought I looked like a pink butterfly in my chiffon dress, and wearing the parasol he bought me, he doesn't realise that pretty pink butterflies can't survive in a climate like they have in Strasbourg. No, within months I would be in dark brown wool, and purple bombazine, and probably black velvet for parties. And the climate I was telling you about, that's very important. Here, a few grey days, a few rainstorms, and I feel ready to cry for the rest of my life. Imagine me there in the freezing winters, and the long, wet autumn afternoons."

"You could have a log fire," said Naomi, "and wear a fur coat."

"It wouldn't be enough. I should be chilly all the way through. And then of course, there's you girls. How can I leave you, and not see you for years and years?"

"We could visit you," said Naomi.

"For how long? And how often, even if Max were willing to pay? I would miss seeing you grow up, and I don't think I could bear that. And the city. I know every stone and corner, and all my life I've never even thought about them, but never to see an olive tree again, never to walk in the market, where everyone knows me, never to see my friends again, the friends I grew up with—no, I couldn't bear it. I shall write to Max tonight and tell him. It's not fair to wait until the last moment."

"Poor Max," said Rifka, "won't he be heartbroken?"

"Heartbroken? No, I don't think so. Upset at first, and very angry that his plans have been spoiled, but in the end, he, too, will realise it's for the best, and probably marry a plump Strasbourg widow of his acquaintance, whom he mentioned to me while he was here. No, I don't think he will be heartbroken, and anyway, I don't propose, fond as I am of Max, and much as I will miss him in many ways, to break my heart with loneliness just so that he can be happy. That's something all you girls should learn now, before you are grown-up. Never sacrifice yourselves. You'll only become bitter and resentful. Do what is right for you."

"That sounds selfish," said Rifka. "I thought you were supposed to be kind to everyone."

"Kind to everyone, and to yourself too. You are just as import-ant as anybody else, Rifka, and it's something you, in particular, shouldn't forget. Already you stay late in the shop on Friday after-noon just because Mrs. Gluckmann has to prepare her Sabbath. Tell her one day, you have to leave early. See what happens. She probably won't mind at all, and you will have been sacrificing yourself for nothing."

Rifka was silent. "I'm glad you're not leaving, Mimi. It would have been terrible, you and David both going at the same time.

Now you'll be here, and we can still visit you, just as we always have."

"And who," said Chava, laughing, "will look after you in your old age?"

Mimi threw back her head and laughed, too. "Why, you will, Chavale darling, just as you once said you would, remember? And I shall be a lovely great aunt for your children . . ."

". . . and feed them Turkish Delight and sugared almonds," added Naomi.

". . . and tell them stories about Chava, and how she was when she was little," said Rifka.

". . . and fall asleep in your chair, like old Mrs. Levinsky, when people come to call," said Chava. "It will be fun."

"But meanwhile there's still tonight," said Mimi, "and that letter. I've been composing it in my head for days, and it never sounds right. I must do it now, and have done with the whole matter—it's a weight on my mind. I wish I could write easily, like Naomi. I have to squeeze every word out painfully, even at the best of times, but on occasions like this, when what I say really matters, I'm completely bewildered."

"Never mind, Mimi," said Chava, "do it now, and you'll feel better. Give yourself a treat when you've finished, and if you hold the treat in your mind while you're writing, you'll do it much more quickly."

"Crafty Chava, what a good idea! No dinner till it's done. I've put a casserole on the stove that smells delicious—can you all smell it? Isn't it lovely? And not a morsel shall pass my lips till Max's letter is written."

"I suppose," said Rifka, "talking of letters, there has been nothing for us from the Rabbi's brother?"

"Don't you know that if something came from America, I would run and give it to you, whatever else I was doing?" said

Mimi.

"Yes, of course," said Rifka, "only you must be very careful not to let Mother, or anyone, know. That's why we gave your address. I don't know what she would do if she saw an American stamp, and the letter was not from Isaac."

"Don't worry," said Mimi. "Not a word will I breathe, and if I have to come to your house suddenly, I'll think of some excuse. I only wish he would hurry. I will feel easier in my mind when I know your photograph has crossed the ocean safely and is at least in the same country as Isaac. And now, my darlings, you must go home. I promised your mother I wouldn't keep you late."

"And you," said Chava, "must write that letter."

"Yes," said Mimi dolefully, "and no supper till I've finished. Oh dear." She looked hopefully at the girls as they put on their jackets. "Couldn't I have just the tiniest slice of cake to give me courage?"

"No," said Rifka, Chava and Naomi in a chorus. "Not a bite until you've finished."

"Maybe I'll marry him after all," said Mimi. "It might be less trouble in the end! No, I'm only teasing. I'll do it if it kills me. Now kiss me, and go quickly and make sure Shoshie doesn't jump in the puddles on the way home. Your mother would never forgive me."

As soon as the girls had gone, Mimi sat down at her desk, took out a sheet of paper, a pen, and an inkwell, and began to write:

My dearest Max,

I am not going to find this letter easy to write. I have been thinking what to say and how to say it for many days now, ever since I came to my decision, and there is only one way to do it,

and that is to say frankly what I want to say at the very beginning. I can't marry you. There, I've written it, and you've read
it, and the worst is over. (Perhaps, thought Mimi, I could have a
salted almond? Just one? No, press on. There's a lot more to say.)
Believe me, dear Max, that I know what I am saying. I must
apologise to you, and ask your pardon for behaving in this silly
way, like a young girl, instead of thinking, and having the sense,
while you were here, to see that I could never be happy away
from my home, my family, my friends, and my country. (That's
well put, thought Mimi. Quite stirring those words sound, just
like a book. Maybe it won't be as bad as I feared.) Of course, I
shall miss you, and will always keep happy memories of your
stay, and of the wonderful times we had together. (Well, they
were pleasant, Mimi said to herself, even though my feet were
swollen every night from walking, and my head was bursting
with information about this and that, that I'm not really interested in.) But I think, on mature reflection (I'm sure I've seen
that phrase in a book. Yes, that's just the right thing to say) that
I am not, at my age, ready to submit to the discipline and unsel-
fishness that marriage demands and deserves. (Salted almonds
indeed! That last sentence deserves a three-course meal all by
itself. Brilliant! I can see, thought Mimi, that I'm becoming
quite good at this.) I also know that a man of your discernment
and intelligence (And what man could ever resist a little flat-
tery?) will understand my decision, and someone as kind and
loving as you are, will forgive me. I pray that you will find
someone more worthy than I am to share your lovely home,
and the pleasant twilight of your days. (Poetry! That's what it
is, pure poetry. I never knew that I was capable of such things.
I'm enjoying this, said Mimi to herself, more than I thought
possible. Poor Max, he won't enjoy reading it, I'm afraid. Shall
I say something else, or will anything else spoil the effect? Well,

perhaps just a tiny bit more . . .)

I would like to assure you . . . (no, that sounds like a lawyer.
I'll start again.) I hope you will always remember that I think of
you with the deepest and sincerest affection, and that I will cher-
ish all the memories I have of you until my dying day.

Please find it in your heart to forgive

Your loving and repentant

Mimi

"There," said Mimi aloud, "it's done." She took an envelope
and addressed it, and then read the letter again, pleased at the way
it had turned out. Really, Max should be honoured to receive such
a masterpiece. The fragrance of the casserole hung on the air. Mimi
folded the letter carefully, put it into the envelope, and put the envelope on the table, ready to be posted the next day. Then gathering about her the floating skirts of her peignoir, she swept
triumphantly into the kitchen.

Chapter IX

Mrs. Gluckmann was sitting in the little room behind the shop, checking the accounts for the previous week. Her shoes, new and still tight and stiff, were on the floor under the table, and as her pencil passed over the rows of figures on the page in front of her, she wriggled her stockinged toes about in the air, and sighed with pleasure. From time to time, she dipped her bagel into the glass of tea at her elbow, and took a bite from it, being careful not to drip on to her work, nor scatter crumbs on the page. Rifka, she knew, would deal competently with any customers who came in, and the early afternoon was, anyway, a quiet time. There was no reason for her to hurry, and remembering the agony of the new shoes, every reason to spend the best part of the afternoon sitting comfortably at her table.

Rifka, perched on the stool behind the counter, was hemming a handkerchief, ready to embroider for Dvora's birthday. Most of the bread had been sold in the morning, but there were still cakes and pastries left, and another two hours before she could think about going home. None of the early spring sunlight came through the small windows of the shop at this hour of the day, but it cheered Rifka to look out at the houses across the street, on which the sun was shining, and above them, she could make out a pale blue triangle of sky. Spring was coming, the best time, the warm flower-filled, blossom-filled season that lasted for so few weeks before the burning summer heat arrived, and baked the earth, and dried the flowers up, and made people cross and tired. What will it be like here, Rifka thought, in the summer? It was lovely in the cold weather, smelling the new bread, each loaf still giving off its own oven warmth, but in summer, and with those windows, I'll suffocate. And the cakes, with all that sticky sugar and honey: how will I keep the flies away? There hasn't been anyone in the shop for a long time now, maybe half an hour. If no-one comes for a little while longer, I'll finish this, and tonight I'll ask Mother for some embroidery silk, and make a pattern all round the edge. Flowers, maybe. No, rabbits! Can Naomi draw good rabbits? What shall I do if she can't? Rifka was just beginning to worry about this, when she heard someone tapping on the glass outside. She looked up quickly. It was Mimi. Rifka jumped off the stool, and began to open her mouth to speak, when she saw Mimi grimacing at her through the glass, her finger to her lips and a deep frown on her face. Rifka mouthed the word "Why?" silently, and was quite mystified to see Mimi glancing quickly to each side, as if to make certain no-one had seen her. She opened the door of the shop as quietly as she possibly could, wincing dramatically at every tiny creak. Then she stood just inside the door, with one hand on the handle, ready to flee, and beckoned to Rifka.

"What is it?" whispered Rifka. "What's the matter? Why are you acting like a robber?"

"Where is she?" Mimi hissed. "Mrs. Gluckmann?"

"In the back, doing the accounts. It's alright, she always has some tea and something to eat and takes ages and ages. Anyway, why are you hiding from Aunt Zehava? I thought you quite liked her."

"I do quite like her, and her cakes I like even more, but I've got a letter here."

"A letter?" For a moment, Rifka was confused.

"From America. From the Rabbi's brother . . . Ssh!" she added, as Rifka opened her mouth wide, ready to shout for joy. She remembered in time, and covered her mouth with both hands as she hopped up and down with excitement like a small child.

"Where is it?"

"Here. I came as soon as I could." Mimi took the envelope from her handbag, and gave it to Rifka. "Aren't you going to open it?"

"Yes, yes, of course I am. I just . . ."

"Reefka!" came a shout from the back room, and Mimi froze. "What's happening out there? I can hear all kinds of strange noises."

"Nothing, Aunt Zehava," said Rifka, as Mimi opened the door, and slipped quickly into the street, waving a hurried goodbye to Rifka. "Nothing, really. I was muttering to myself, that's all."

"Muttering?" Mrs. Gluckmann sounded doubtful, as if muttering was an occupation to which she had not given much consideration. "Well, if muttering is what you want to do, and there are no customers, then I see no reason . . . but I heard a jumping noise, too."

"Yes, that was me, too," Rifka shouted back, impatient to go back to her stool and read the letter. "I was hopping up and down."

"Hopping? Muttering and hopping. Ah well!" Mrs. Gluckmann sighed. "You young people, I don't know where you find the energy."

Rifka said, "Can I bring you something else? A bun, maybe, or a marzipan pastry?"

"Thank you, child, but no," said Mrs. Gluckmann. "Every cake I eat seems to go straight to my feet. They've doubled in size in the last hour, I could swear they had."

"You need to rest them," Rifka said cunningly. "You should put them up on the stool for a while, that'll make them feel better."

"What a good idea," said Mrs. Gluckmann. "I think I'll do that for a few minutes, and then I'll come in and help you with the evening rush."

Rifka waited for a few moments until heavy, quiet breathing from the back room told her that Mrs. Gluckmann was dozing, as Rifka had known she would. She took the needle she had been using, and used it to tear open the envelope. As quietly as she could, for she did not want the rustling of paper to disturb Mrs. Gluckmann, she laid the pages flat on the counter in front of her, and began to read:

New York,
December 6th, 1913

Dear Miss Bernstein,

Never before in my life—and I am quite an old man—have I had a letter quite like yours. You could have knocked me down with a feather, as the young people here say all the time. So you think I can find your brother, do you? And my brother, the Rabbi, thinks so too? Well, you flatter me, you really do. At first, I was inclined to write a stern letter back to you, telling you to forget such nonsense, and that to look for your brother here, in a city this size, would be like searching for a needle in a haystack, as they say. But then I looked at you, and your sisters in the photograph, with your pretty dresses and your worried eyes, and that ridiculous fur rug at your feet, and I knew I had to try, at least, to help you. And my wife agreed. In fact, if I'm to tell the whole truth, it was she who urged me—urged? What am I saying?—who forced me, to help you as much as I can. When she read your letter, and looked at you all, dressed up with ribbons in your hair, she shed a few tears, which, I can tell you, is not something she often does. The last time she cried was at the Greenblatt wedding. She says, because the service was so beautiful, but I know it was because she wanted the Greenblatt boy for our daughter. I'm digressing. So where was I? Yes, she wept, and she said to me: "Rube," (that's what they call me in America, not Reuben) "It's your duty to find this Isaac Bernstein, and when you find him, drag him here by his collar, and I'll see to it, believe me, that he writes to that poor mother of his!" And if I find him, which I will tell you about in a moment, then see to it she certainly will. My Pearl is a woman of her word.

So then, I thought about it, and thought about it. Where to go to look for your brother? First, I turned over in my mind some Isaacs of my acquaintance, like the tailor round the corner, and the grocer on the next block, but besides being, all of them, at least fifty years old, not one was called Bernstein. So that was no good. Then I thought of Bernsteins: my dentist, and a very good jeweller doing well in a shop quite near Central Park, but they were also too old, and besides, neither of them was an Isaac. So I concluded that I was not personally acquainted with your brother. This, of course, as you must realise, makes my task of finding him more difficult. But I am not someone who gives up easily, and even if I were, Pearl is someone who never gives up at all, so the long and the short of it is, I have made various enquiries. I regret to tell you that none of them has so far been a success. My friend who owns a garment factory has taken on a dozen new machine operatives, but no Isaac Bernstein. I have spoken to three Rabbis, to ask if there is an Isaac Bernstein in their congregation. There is, in every case, and it is always someone who could not possibly be your brother. One was a poor, shrivelled creature with a grey face and spongy hands working in the steam room of a laundry. I showed him your picture, but he shook his head, and went on pressing trousers in a thick, hot fog. Another was a skinny specimen who didn't seem to have any employment, but lay around in the cafés all day. He said he was trying to be a poet. He admired you all, but did not recognise the faces. Then there was a little butcher's assistant who wiped his bloodstained hands on his apron all the time, and told me that he was an only child, so that was no good. I was, as they say, running up a blind alley.

Then Pearl and I talked it over, and she reminded me that my friend Chaim works here for the Yiddish newspaper.

"You should print," she says, "the picture in the newspaper, and have underneath a touching story about the mother and the sisters, and ask anyone knowing of any Isaac Bernstein to come to the newspaper office and tell."

I laughed at her. I said: "So now you're William Randolph Hearst!" (In case you don't know of him, he is the owner of many American newspapers.) "Chaim can't say what picture is to be printed where. That is for the Editor to say. Maybe they have important news to print, and no room for the photograph?"

"What," says Pearl, "is more important than a family eating its heart out with grief? You go and see Chaim tomorrow, because if you don't, I will, and if I do, he'll wish he'd never set foot on the boat from Lithuania." This, I could believe, so I went the next day to see Chaim, and showed him your letter and the photograph, and told him the whole story. He was touched, believe me.

"I'll write it up myself, Rube," he said, "and we'll print it the minute we have the space, I promise you. It's the kind of story that tugs at the heartstrings." Those were his very words.

And so, there you are, dear Miss Bernstein. We are now waiting. Nothing has appeared yet. Pearl says to wait a week, and then go and nag Chaim a little more, or the "touching story" will end up at the bottom of some file. As soon as your picture

121

appears, I feel sure, things will begin to happen. I will, in any case, send you the newspaper cutting, so that you can see it, because it's not every day that you have your picture in the paper for everyone to see.

Meanwhile, be strong and of a good courage, as it says in the Bible, and Pearl and I send you our good wishes, and to your mother and sisters, too, and we will write and tell you as soon as we have any news.

Sincerely yours,
Reuben Mann

Rifka finished reading the letter and folded it back into the envelope. Her hands were trembling, and she had to sit down very quickly on the stool, because she felt so dizzy. Their picture in a newspaper! Wait, wait, till I show this to Chava and Naomi, she said to herself. They won't believe it. I can hardly believe it. That Pearl sounds so clever. Oh, why, why, why does the time go by so slowly? I want to go home. I want to go home now.

Chapter X

Picnics, thought Mimi, who needs them? Why can't they sit on chairs in houses, and eat from plates, like civilised people? Why risk ants, flies, red earth on every garment, and a sunburned nose, even in April? Sarah's idea of a treat. She must be mad. And what am I supposed to wear? Something that I won't miss if it's ruined. The flowered muslin? It's so old, I can't remember when I last wore it, therefore it's sure to be out of style. Still, I refuse to risk the pink lawn just in order to impress—who? My own family and the Levinskys, that's who. No, the flowered muslin it will be, with the Leghorn hat. I'll put such a bunch of flowers at the side of the crown that no-one will even think of looking at my dress. The food is in the basket, ready. Cold chickens and pickled cucumbers, and I even made a great effort and baked those little triangular pastries filled with salty cheese. I can never remember what Ruhama calls them—burrekas, that's it. Delicious. I suppose if everyone brings enough good food it won't be so bad, but who needs it? Still, it's the last time Rifka will see David before he leaves, so I shall try and put a smile on, and make it a happy day. I must practise my smile a little: it feels stiff.

Mimi looked into her mirror and was quite pleasantly surprised at the sight of herself in the wide-brimmed straw hat. The smile she saw reflected in the glass became perceptibly brighter.

I never wanted today to come, thought Rifka, as she struggled to plait Dvora's hair while Dvora was jumping up and down in excitement. I didn't want it to come, and now it's here I wish it would go away. I wish I could go to sleep, and wake up yesterday, and have all the days going backwards for a while. Tomorrow he'll be gone, and I won't see him for two years. Seven hundred and thirty days, Chava worked it out. Everyone says that the time will fly, but it never does, never, not till it's gone, and then it seems to have flown. It's slow while it's going on. I don't feel festive and picknicky. The others have hardly slept for three nights talking about it, and looking forward to it, and Shoshie is going to sit next to the driver and look at the mule for ages, all the way to Abu Gosh, nearly. Mother has been baking and cooking for days, the postman's brother is driving us in the cart he uses for bringing his fruit into the market, and Mrs. Gluckmann is looking after the shop alone, just for a treat, and she has made quite sure I know how kind she's being by mentioning it twenty times a day for the past fortnight. She wipes an imaginary tear from her eye from time to time, also, just to show how sympathetic she is to "young love and its problems", as she calls it. I wish it were all over already. I feel a little sick.

"Dvora," she snapped, "how can I do your hair when you're jumping up and down. Keep still, for goodness' sake!" The unusual anger in her sister's voice made Dvora stand very quietly, and she looked at Rifka's frowning face, not understanding.

Sarah was on the balcony, counting baskets on her fingers: "Food, cushions, drinks, sewing . . ." I hope I've made enough for everyone. Mrs. Levinsky said she'll bring, and Mimi, too, but who knows how much? Will the cart be here soon? It's late already. Is Rifka dealing with the little ones? Let me just count the baskets again.

David looked at his trunk, all packed and ready, standing at the foot of his bed. Tomorrow, it would be on the boat. I wish this picnic were over, he thought. How will I say goodbye? What will I say? Will Rifka cry? I hope she doesn't, yet perhaps I hope she does. At least I have the photograph to take with me.

My only son is leaving tomorrow, thought Mrs. Levinsky, cutting a plum tart into squares, and wrapping the squares carefully in a clean cloth. He's leaving tomorrow, and I'm supposed to go and sparkle and enjoy myself, without even my husband to help, because he, of course, is safely at his work. Ah, well, that's being a mother—nothing but anguish. Anguish and cooking, anguish and cleaning, anguish and washing and ironing. My poor little boy, all alone in a strange country. Have I made enough plum tart, I wonder, for all those girls?

Grandfather Levinsky knotted his cravat, hummed a waltz under his breath, and tried to feel sorry that his wife was being left behind in the care of a neighbour. Déjeuner sur l'herbe . . . fête champêtre . . . ah, those were the days. Picnics on fresh young grass in the soft countryside around Paris. Fresh young women, too, and cold chicken legs and champagne. And here? Rugs spread on the red earth in the very slender shade of a cypress tree. Why am I going? Because I like outings and good food, and for David's sake on his last day. And, of course (admit it!) to get away from my wife who has turned into an old lady. It wasn't always so. Grandfather Levinsky sighed regretfully, and turned his mind to happier matters.

Everything is going so well, thought Naomi, tying the ribbons of her hat under her chin. First, the letter from the Rabbi's brother, although that was nearly two months ago, and now a picnic. Why doesn't the picture of us in the newspaper come? Will Isaac see it? Does he read newspapers? I wish he could come with us today. I shall write and tell him all about it.

"No," said Mrs. Gluckmann to her first customer of the day, "I'm all on my own today. Rifka is going on a picnic. Well, I don't normally let my employees take days away from work whenever the fancy takes them, but where young love is concerned, who can be strict? Her betrothed leaves for Europe tomorrow, so for one day, I'll kill my poor feet, and with pleasure. After all, the way I think of it is this: she'll have no distractions from her work for the next two years."

They're always awful, thought Chava, and we always remember them as lovely, and go back for more. Shoshie eats too much and is sick on the way home, you have to watch Dvora like a hawk in case she wanders away, Mimi fusses about her clothes. I wish I could stay here with a book. Rifka will probably faint in the sunshine, even though it's not hot. She looks like a ghost already, and David hasn't even gone yet. What will she be like next week?

I wish we could take the cat, thought Dvora, sitting on the top step, waiting for everyone to be ready. He'll be all alone here all day. Who will look after him? Mother says cats don't come on picnics, but I don't see why not. She says he'll get lost, but I say we could tie a ribbon round his neck. Chava says it's cruel, but I don't think it's cruel. I'd give him half my food. Perhaps I'll take him down to the Old Man. They can keep each other company. Dvora got up, and went to look for the cat.

My dolls are coming on the picnic, thought Shoshie. Naomi has made them new clothes. They've promised to be very good. I've also promised to be good, and I wish I hadn't now.

For a long time, the mule-cart jogged along the road out of the city and began to wind its way around the curves of hills and into deep, terraced valleys. Squashed on to the benches along the side of the cart were eleven people, and probably, thought the postman's brother, double that number of baskets. It's no wonder my poor mule is breathless. So many children are sitting on so many laps, it's a puzzle to me how they'll disentangle themselves when we get there.

At last, everyone was sitting down on blankets in the sun. Sarah Bernstein heaved a sigh of relief. They had arrived in one piece.

"We always come here," she said. "This line of trees makes a pleasant shade, and the children used to play such games in that old, white house over there, you wouldn't believe it. It's a ruin really, of course, no roof and only three and a half walls, but you can see it must once have been lovely. There are even the remains of a garden. Look, a peach tree against that wall, and vines running wild, and still some bougainvillaea climbing in at the window."

"I always pretend it's a ruined castle," said Naomi.

"You would," said Chava, under her breath.

"And look at the view from here," said Mimi bravely to Grandfather Levinsky. "Wasn't it worth the journey just for the view?"

"Madam," replied the old man staring at Mimi's hat, "the view from where I sit is utterly delightful. I haven't seen such a pretty view in years. How is it I have never seen it before?" He winked, and Mimi blushed.

David and Rifka sat next to one another and said nothing. Shoshie had put her dolls to sleep on a nearby boulder. Sarah and Mrs. Levinsky were already opening the baskets, and placing plates and cutlery in neat rows that wobbled a little on the uneven ground.

"Mimi, you've made burrekas, you darling!" shouted Chava. "You know how I love them." And she took one in each hand and began to nibble at them.

"Wait, Chava, wait for everyone to start together," said Sarah.

"But what's the point of having a picnic at all," said Chava, "if we have to bring our table manners with us?"

"I can see you've left yours safe at home," said Mrs. Levinsky with an icy smile.

"But I know," replied Chava sweetly, "that they'll be waiting for me when I get back." She helped herself to another burreka.

David said to Rifka: "I've packed your photograph in my trunk."

Rifka said: "Is your trunk packed already?"

"Yes," said David. "Mother didn't want to leave anything until after the picnic. She said we'd be too tired."

"I expect you will be," said Rifka.

"But I don't think I'll be able to sleep," said David. "Not to-night."

"No," said Rifka. "I don't think I will, either."

"But then how will you manage in the shop tomorrow?" David sounded anxious.

"Doesn't matter, the shop doesn't matter," muttered Rifka, so quietly that David had to lean forward to catch what she was saying.

"Now come," shouted Sarah, "fill up your plates, everyone, and enjoy the food. Rifka, will you pour the lemonade?" She held up two large stone bottles, and Rifka rose from her place beside David and went to take them.

Grandfather Levinsky opened his eyes and caught sight of Mimi. "I think I must have died, and I suppose this must be Heaven," he said.

"What nonsense you talk!" Mimi laughed. "You've been asleep. Too much food and sunshine."

"Forty winks, my dear, forty winks. An old man's privilege. Forgive me."

"Of course," said Mimi, thinking privately that it had been nearer sixty winks. For hours, it seemed, she had been gazing at the picturesque, but extremely boring view. Nature, she had decided, was vastly overrated, and as she removed stone after little stone from where she was sitting, she thought longingly of plush chaises-longues, and pretty lampshades and soft, soft beds.

"Perhaps," said Grandfather Levinsky, struggling to his feet, "you would care for a short promenade, Madame."

"Why, that would be delightful," said Mimi, and jumped up as eagerly as a young girl, wishing she had worn stouter shoes. Together, they made their way down the path to the next line of cypress trees.

"Rifka hardly ate anything," said Sarah to Mrs. Levinsky. "I'm afraid she'll miss him dreadfully."

"He'll miss her, too, at first," said Mrs. Levinsky, "but then, of course, he'll be busy with his studies, and meeting new people . . ."

Sarah was silent. It was her secret terror, that she had hugged to herself through many nights, that David would meet some wealthy young heiress, who happened also to be Jewish and beautiful, and leave Rifka for ever. After all, there had been no formal marriage contract. Sarah sometimes pictured Europe as being populated entirely by rich and beautiful young girls, waiting for their chance to snatch David away from her daughter. She prayed every night that this should not be so, but where Rifka and David were concerned, she was not sure that she altogether trusted God.

Rifka and David stood in the ruined house, looking out of a window with no glass.

"Sometimes," said Rifka "you can see people riding mules or donkeys along that road up there, bringing fruit and vegetables to the city in big baskets."

"Will you write to me?" said David.

"What will I say? Nothing much happens to me."

"It doesn't matter. You can tell me about things you do, and things you think. And about what happens with the Rabbi's brother, and Isaac."

"Maybe nothing will happen."

"But you told me it was such a nice letter, and that he was going to put your picture in the newspaper."

"Yes," said Rifka, "yes, it was nice, but we haven't heard for such a long time, so maybe nothing will happen after all."

"I'll write to you."

"Yes, please," said Rifka. "I've never had letters just for me alone. And you'll see so many interesting things."

"I'd rather stay here with you."

"Really?"

"Really."

"I'm glad."

"Rifka, you will wait for me, won't you?"

"Wait for you? Where would I go without you?"

"I don't mean go anywhere, I mean . . ."

"I know what you mean." Rifka smiled. "You don't have to worry. I'll wait for you."

"And I'll come back. It seems like a long time, but it'll go quickly, you'll see, with letters."

"I hope it does."

"Rifka, will you let me kiss you goodbye?"

"Kiss me?" Rifka began to tremble.

"Yes." David stepped forward, and took Rifka's hands. "Like this," and his lips rested on hers briefly, like a breeze, like a butterfly, and then were gone.

"I think we should go back to the others now," said Rifka, confused and blushing. "They'll wonder where we are."

"Then give me your hand," said David, and together they walked down the sloping path to where the rest of the company were sitting.

"Hide and seek," said Dvora. "Please play."

"We might as well," said Naomi. "David and Rifka have disappeared into the ruined house, Mimi has gone for a walk with Grandfather Levinsky, and Mother and Mrs. Levinsky are gossiping."

"I wish I'd brought something to read," said Chava.

"Come and play with us," said Naomi.

"Very well," Chava sighed, "but hide and seek with Dvora and Shoshie is so boring. Shoshie always hides in the same place over and over again, and expects us to fall over in surprise when we find her. And we're expected not to notice bits of Dvora sticking out from behind rocks and trees that are too small for her."

"Come on," said Naomi, "just for once. What have you got to do that's better?"

"Nothing," said Chava, brushing bits of earth from her skirt as she stood up. She followed Naomi up the hill to where the best hiding-places were to be found.

"They'll never find us here," said Dvora, with a smug smile as she and Shoshie flattened themselves behind two rocks that stood close together. In the distance, she could hear Naomi's voice saying: "Well, they've really hidden themselves away this time. I do hope we can find them." Shoshie wriggled, delighted at the hiding and being found at last. When Naomi put her head over the top of the rock and said: "Goodness, look who is hiding here!" she jumped up at once and said: "Again! Do it again!" and Chava and Naomi obediently covered their eyes.

The baskets are lighter now, thought the postman's brother as the cart creaked towards Jerusalem at sunset, and the people are heavier. The little girls are asleep now, on their sisters' laps, so it's altogether quieter than this morning. That old man seems to have found a friend, and who can blame him? She's a fine figure of a woman, that. I'd like to see my Rachel in her hat! The driver chuckled to himself, and patted his mule affectionately.

Chava moved her knees into a more comfortable position, and held the sleeping Dvora against her shoulder. We will drive into the city just as the light is leaving the sky, she thought. It wasn't such a bad picnic. The little ones behaved, and now they're like small pink angels in the sunset. Dvora is a very heavy angel. My legs will be numb before we get home.

When I have to part from someone I love, thought Naomi, I shall see to it that we're alone. How is she going to say goodbye to him in front of all of us? Mimi gets out first, then us, and the Levinskys last of all. Funny, she doesn't look so sad now. More dreamy. David hasn't said a word since we set out for home. They haven't stopped holding hands all day. It's so romantic.

Grandfather Levinsky felt good. Pleasant food, pleasant wine, and very pleasant company. Quite an enjoyable picnic, thanks to Mimi. A mature woman, but with style and wit, and a good figure still. A very good figure. Grandfather Levinsky tried to concentrate on Mimi, but as they approached the city, he began to think of his wife more and more. The picnic was over.

Moshe will want to hear every detail, thought Mrs. Levinsky, and I'll have to tell him, even though it's David's last night. A not unpleasant day, after all, better than I expected, and my plum tart was much admired. I've never known a child to eat like that Chava. I'm glad David isn't marrying her, she's too clever. I pity any husband of hers. Rifka now, is a good girl. I don't think she'll give me any trouble.

We've said goodbye already, thought David, so this doesn't count. I won't be able to say anything at all, let alone tell Rifka how I feel. Does she know? Have I told her properly? Perhaps in letters I'll be able to say things I can't say to her face. It's nearly dark now and I can't see her eyes.

A success, thought Sarah, a lovely day, a day for Rifka to remember when he's gone. My poor child, my lovely girl, I know, I remember how you feel, and I'd like to hug you and hold you and comfort you, just like a baby. Yes, I know exactly how you feel, although for me, it was many years ago.

I can hear the wheels turning, thought Rifka, and the mule clattering along the road. And I can hear my own heart. But we kissed. If I shut my eyes and concentrate hard, I can remember exactly what it felt like, and how he looked, his eyes when he kissed me. How long will it be before I forget what he looked like at that moment?

Thank God that's over, thought Mimi. I've eaten too much, and my feet are sore, and I've flirted with that nice old man, and now it's over and we can all go back to normal. The sooner David leaves the better: this ride now is just prolonging the agony. If Rifka were my daughter, he would have come to the house, said goodbye, and left. Poor child! I wonder if there are any young men she could meet to cheer her a little while he's away. I'll ask Ruhama. Heaven help us if she has to spend two years in this state.

As soon as she closed the door of the flat behind her, Mimi took off her shoes and went into the bedroom to take off the hat, and put on some loose clothes. When she emerged in a flowing lacy nightdress, she noticed a letter lying on the floor beside the door. It was addressed to Rifka, and Mimi recognised the writing of the Rabbi's brother at once, and went happily to put the letter under the copper vase until the morning. No-one can say, she thought, that God isn't merciful. Here he sends a letter from America on the very day that Rifka needs it, to take her mind off David. I will be at the shop tomorrow the minute it opens. Or maybe that's a little early, eight o'clock in the morning. I'll go as soon as I wake up. Pleased at the thought of Rifka's smile, Mimi went into the kitchen to see what she could find for supper. The picnic had been delicious, but that was quite a long time ago.

Much later that night, when the others were asleep, Rifka left her room, and went into the little girls' bedroom. She picked Shoshie up in her arms, and carried her, still asleep, into her own bed. Lying in the dark, cuddled up to Shoshie for comfort, she looked at the ceiling, and cried very quietly, so as not to wake her sisters.

Chapter XI

"We must hide the cutting very carefully," said Rifka. "If the little ones find it, they're sure to say something about it to Mother."

"Let me have one last look at it before you put it away," said Naomi, and she unfolded the piece of newspaper and spread it out on her bed.

"I can't think what's so interesting," said Chava. "It's only the photograph after all. You can look at it every day on our sideboard."

"But it's different in a newspaper—more important and dignified somehow. And look what it says underneath." Naomi began to read the few lines printed under their picture: "'Do *you* know these lovely young girls? Somewhere in this city there is a young man who is their brother. His name is Isaac Bernstein, and if he will present himself at these offices, there is a pleasant surprise waiting for him. Isaac, wherever you are, please come forward!' I suppose the pleasant surprise is our letters?"

"I hope Isaac thinks it's worth the journey. *If* he sees the newspaper, of course," said Chava.

"But how can he miss it?" Naomi sounded tearful.

"Easily. You forget that newspapers only last one day, and then what happens to them? They're used to wrap vegetables in, or to line cupboards, or light fires, or else they simply collect in a pile in a corner somewhere. All Isaac has to do is *not* read the newspaper for one day, and he will have missed us."

"I never thought of it like that," said Naomi quietly, and turned her face away, so that Chava shouldn't see the beginnings of tears in her eyes.

"Mr. Mann seems quite hopeful," said Rifka.

"He's that sort of person," said Chava. "You can tell from his letters. He would look on the bright side of things, whatever happened. Read the letter again and you'll see."

"Would you like me to read it aloud, Naomi?" Rifka knew very well what Naomi's surreptitious sniffing was all about.

"Yes, please."

"Very well, then listen." Rifka began to read.

"To dear Miss Rifka and her lovely sisters, greetings. Now, as you can see from the cutting I have enclosed, we are really getting somewhere, as they say. Pearl was quite right, and I had to visit my friend in the newspaper offices quite frequently in order to hurry him along and jog his memory. Pearl even sent him a cheesecake, and that seemed to do the trick, as you might say, because one week after the cheesecake, on February 17th, here you are for all the world to see. Good cheesecake, I knew it was, but now it has turned out to be almost magical. I'm sure it will not be long now before your brother writes to you. He is sure to see your picture in the paper (it has an enormous circulation) and even if he doesn't, someone in his place of work, wherever that is, will read what it says, and tell Isaac. I was very insistent that the name should be mentioned.

Please, when you hear from him, write and tell me. I would like to know that you have done what you set out to do, and besides, Pearl and I have become quite caught up in your problem, and will feel easier when it has a happy ending. If my brother ever asks after us we are well. I know the cares of his holy office make it hard for him to write, but we would love to have news of him, please tell him. Now there's a funny thing. It has only just occurred to me that we are, as they say, in the same boat! Each trying to get a brother to write to us. But at least I know where mine is, so I suppose that makes it a little different.

It will be spring, probably, when this letter reaches you. I've been in this country for many years now, but I haven't forgotten what Palestine in April is like. Here, you're lucky if you see a tree, unless it's in the park. My regards to your mother, and best wishes from Reuben Mann. P.S. Pearl also wishes to send her kind regards. A pity, I said, she couldn't send some cheesecake as well." Rifka paused. "I think that's a nice letter. I think he's a very nice man. And when Isaac writes to us, I shall write and thank him."

"If," said Chava.

"If what?"

"If Isaac writes. Not *when* Isaac writes."

Rifka smiled. "You're such a pessimist, Chava. Why do you always expect the worst?"

"Because if you do," said Chava, "the nice things come as a wonderful surprise, and the bad things don't hurt so badly."

Rifka took the newspaper cutting from Naomi's bed, and folded it into the envelope with the letter.

"Where can I hide this?" she asked. "Mother is easy, she hardly ever looks in our drawers, but Dvora and Shoshie are everywhere."

"Put it behind the drawer itself," said Chava. "Take the whole drawer out, and put the letter right next to the back of the chest of drawers, and then put the drawer in again. No-one will think of looking for it there."

"That's a good idea," said Rifka. "Clever Chava. I'll do it straightaway. Stand by the door to make sure no-one comes while we're doing it."

Chava went and stood by the open door, and looked into the

137

courtyard. She could see Dvora and Shoshie and Menahem lining up little stones in elaborate patterns on the ground. In their hutch, the rabbits twitched their ears, and no-one took any notice at all.

"It's funny, isn't it?" said Chava over her shoulder, "how the rabbits are no longer so exciting now that Menahem has become friendly, and said the girls can feed them whenever they like. He hardly looks at them either." She laughed. "Poor little creatures! Before, they were in danger of eating themselves to death, and now they're probably going to die of starvation. Can I come in again now, Rifka?"

"Yes, come in. The letter is safely hidden," said Rifka.

"And now," said Naomi sadly, "we just have to sit and wait."

Chapter XII

SUMMER 1914

Rifka was alone in the kitchen at last. I must read them just once more, she thought, now that the others are busy. David's letters to me. Chava and Naomi were quite upset, when I wouldn't show them, but I don't see why I should. They're private. For me. I've never had anything private for me, ever, and now I have, I don't see why I should tell them. I don't look in Naomi's private notebooks, even though I know it's only poems and stories. I shan't ever show these letters to anyone. She took the letters out of her pocket, and began to read them for the twentieth time. The first one said:

My dearest Rifka,
   I am writing this on the boat. It is very rough and a lot of people are seasick. I thought it would be easy to write to you and tell you things, but it's harder even than talking. Maybe if I write often, I'll get better. I was very sad the night of the picnic at the thought of not seeing you for so long, and I'm missing you. Do you miss me? It's funny on the boat. They have cabins just like little rooms, and also a dining-room where we sit at very grand tables and eat a lot of good food. Maybe one day, we will go on a boat together. Please write to me. Tomorrow we arrive in Naples, and I will send you a letter. Also a postcard of the volcano Vesuvius. Please give my regards to your mother and sisters. To you I send my love and a kiss.
                                    David

Rifka wiped away a tear. Perhaps it wasn't a passionate love-letter, such as Mimi had tied in blue ribbons in her desk, and over whose elaborate phrases the girls had often giggled, but it said everything Rifka wanted. David was sad, and missing her and he sent her his love and a kiss.

The second letter, from Naples, was even better, if a little short. Why doesn't he write more? she thought. Still, anything is lovely. The girls had stuck the postcard of Vesuvius on the mirror in the dining-room, but Rifka didn't mind that. After all, it was addressed to the Bernstein family. She began to read the second letter:

Dearest Rifka,

It was wonderful to get your letter in Naples. You write lovely letters. I felt just as if you were talking to me, and it made me feel you weren't so far away. Please write more. I know you think nothing ever happens to you, but it's good to have stories about the little girls, and descriptions of everything. I wish I could do that. Naples is very beautiful, with shops full of things and wide streets. It is quite hot here already. I dream of you a lot, and then I feel sad when I wake up. Do you ever dream about me? I am counting the days till I see you again. Tomorrow I am going on a train and I'm very excited about that and will tell you about it in my next letter.

All my love to you, and a kiss from
David

All his love. If that isn't a proper love-letter, Rifka thought, then I don't know what is. She began to hum a tune under her breath, and thought about what she would say in her next letter as she started scraping carrots for supper with a light heart.

140

Chapter XIII

"There's the postman," said Chava, leaning out of the window, "coming up the road outside. Look, Naomi."

Naomi knelt on the bed and craned her neck to see.

"He looks worried. Why do you think he's hurrying so?"

"Maybe he's got a letter that's marked 'Urgent'," said Chava.

"Maybe. I wonder who it's for. Perhaps for someone in this house. Rifka, probably. Don't you think it's lovely, the way they write to each other every week?"

Chava wrinkled her nose. "He's only been gone a few months. I expect he'll write less and less as time goes on."

"Why?"

"Because he'll think of Rifka less and less, and think more and more of all the things that are happening there."

"That's not true," Naomi nearly shouted. "They love each other, and it'll get more and more, not less and less. You're horrible to say such a thing. I think you're jealous, that's what I think." She burst into tears, and hid her face in the pillow. Chava shook her by the shoulder.

"Come on, Naomi, for heaven's sake don't be so dramatic. I'm not jealous. What's there to be jealous of? I don't want to get married, and certainly not to David when I'm sixteen. Stop crying. What will they think at school? And breakfast must be ready. Come on, I didn't mean to be horrible, really. Let's go and see what the postman's got for Rifka."

Naomi sat up, and wiped her face with a handkerchief.

"Where are Dvora and Shoshie?" she asked.

"Helping Mother. Come on, we'll go down into the courtyard and wait there."

Sarah was trying to take hardboiled eggs out of a saucepan and put them on a plate without treading on her two youngest daughters, who had come in to help, but had decided that playing fishes all over the floor was pleasanter.

"Do move to another room, Dvora, and play fishes there. How can I cook? And what if I should spill some boiling water by accident?"

"This is the slippiest floor," said Dvora. "Best for fish."

Sarah shook her head, and moved to the table to cut slices of bread. Suddenly, a piercing shriek echoed up from the courtyard, and Sarah dropped the knife.

"Naomi!" she shouted, running out of the room. "That's Naomi! Something's happened. Oh, my God!" She began to clatter down the steps to the courtyard when she saw Naomi and Chava standing perfectly still outside the Friedman house, holding a white envelope. Sarah ran towards them.

"What's the matter? What's happened? Why did you shriek, Naomi?"

Naomi said nothing at first, but put the letter into her mother's hand.

"Look, Mother," she said gently, "it's a letter. A letter from Isaac."

Sarah looked at the envelope in her hands, and turned very pale.

"A letter? From Isaac? How do you know?"

"It says so on the envelope, Mother," said Chava. "Look."

"So it does." Sarah peered at the name, and turned the letter over. "Isaac Bernstein. That's our Isaac." She took a deep breath.

"I must sit down. I think I'm going to faint."

"Then let's go into the house," said Chava. "Come, take my arm, Mother."

They went up the stairs and into the dining-room where Sarah sat beside the table, and stared at the letter in her hand.

"I must open it. I've waited so long for this, I don't know . . . I simply have no courage to open it. Chava, you open it."

"No, Mother, you must. It's addressed to Mrs. Bernstein and the girls. You must open it, but before you do, I want to explain something to you."

"Something bad?" Sarah's voice sharpened in anxiety.

"No, nothing bad," said Chava, and she told her mother about Rifka's letter to the Rabbi's brother, and their letters to Isaac, about how they had sent the photograph, and about the letters from America and the newspaper cutting. Sarah listened in silence, shaking her head from time to time in disbelief.

"Now," said Chava finally, "open the letter."

Sarah took a knife, and slit open the envelope. Chava and Naomi sat down beside her as she began to read aloud in a faltering voice:

"My dearest Mother and sisters,
Picture this scene, if you will. There I am, shivering with cold in the little room I share in this huge cold house with Lev Mendel, a tailor's assistant. I'm even wearing my overcoat and wondering if there's any old wood for the stove, when a knock comes at the door. It's Mrs. Kaminska, the landlady, a dragon in hair curlers, carpet slippers and dirty dresses of no discernible colour. She has, in her hand a damp sheet of newspaper.

"Mrs. Kaminska," I say, "if it's about the rent . . ."

"Rent, rent," she says, "who's talking about rent? I've been cleaning the stairs."

"Good," I say "but why are you telling me?"

"I have to put down newspapers after I clean."

"Yes, I know," (trying not to sound impatient!)

"And this I saw. Why did I look at it? What have I got to do with a picture like this? Believe me when I tell you it reminded me of how I used to look when I was a girl."

"Really?" (I found it so hard to imagine Mrs. K. as a girl that I had difficulty in not laughing.)

"Really," she says. "I want for you to look at the picture. Under is written your name."

"My name?" (Of course, I'd hardly glanced at the newspaper.)

"Isaac Bernstein?"

"Yes," I say, "you know that's my name."

"Well," (triumphantly!) "it says here Isaac Bernstein in black letters."

So I took the paper, and looked at the picture, and nearly fell over when I recognised you all. I kissed Mrs. Kaminska, so you can imagine how excited I was. I ran down the stairs, and walked all the way to the newspaper offices, where I presented myself and was immediately shown into the Editor's office. I wished I could have stayed there overnight, it was so warm. The Editor gave me coffee, and I sat, and sat and read the lovely letters from my darling sisters, and I nearly cried. Then the Editor told me about Reuben Mann, and told me how to get to his house. I went to thank him, of course, for helping you, but I was treated like a son. I ate, as I've not eaten since I left your house, Mother, and then I was urged to eat more. Mr. Mann is very friendly and charming and Mrs. Mann is capable and kind. When I told them about Mrs. Kaminska's rooming house, and the difficulties I had been having trying to find good employment, leaving one boring, underpaid job after another, Mrs.

Mann said:

"Tomorrow you come here. You can lodge with us. Reuben will find you work." Reuben looked doubtful, but she repeated, even more firmly: "Reuben will find you work, won't you, Reuben?" till the poor man was forced to agree. Then I had a bath (Heaven must be one large, hot bath, I think!) and now, dressed in Mr. Mann's old clothes, which are too big for me, she has placed me at the table with a pen and paper, and told me not to move until I have written to you. So here I am. Tomorrow, Reuben will take me to his cousin-in-law, who imports foreign food, and may be able to find me a job either in his warehouse, or as a clerk in his office. His cousin-in-law, he did say, has a daughter, but for all I know, she's worse than Ruthie Gluckmann. I will write about her when I meet her. I *will* write again.

About why I didn't write, I can only say (and it's not really an excuse) that I was waiting for things to get better. I was ashamed to tell you about how homesick and seasick I was on the boat when I had left Jerusalem with such high hopes. Then I came here, and the money came to an end, and every job I had (as dishwasher, waiter, sweeping floors in a garment factory) I was ashamed of telling you about because I thought you would be disappointed. Always I promised myself that the next thing would be better, and that I would write, but it never was. And meanwhile, because of not having money, all I began to think about was how to live from day to day, how to eat, how to keep warm, how to make clothes last. Can you picture me mending my own clothes?

But now, thanks to my sisters and the Manns, everything looks wonderful. A full stomach and clean clothes produce a really beautiful optimism in a person. I feel at this moment like a king. From now on, I know everything will go better, and I will write to you often and without feeling ashamed.

Outside, it's dark now, and I can see a million stars of light in all the windows, and I can hear the wind. I look at your photograph, and it brings a bit of summer into the room, and I can remember the smell of home: the dust, and the pine trees and the ripe fruit. I miss you all and love you, and will write to you often, and you must all write to me. Give my love, too, to Mimi and regards to all friends who remember me. To my sisters, I send kisses and hugs, and to you, Mother, all my love.

Isaac."

Sarah put the letter back into the envelope, then she lowered her head on to her arms and began to weep.

"Mother, Mother, stop," said Naomi. "Why are you crying? It's all alright. It's a happy ending. He's going to be well looked after. He'll write and tell us. Why are you crying? Please stop."

"I'm sorry." Sarah sat up and sniffed. "Only it's too much. My poor boy, all the suffering. Did you hear? No money, not enough to eat! That I should live to hear such things about my son. It's terrible!"

"But it's over, Mother," said Chava. "It's all over now."

"And the good things are just beginning," said Naomi. "He will be rich and ride in carriages soon, just as I always knew he would."

Chava, for once, said nothing. Sarah wiped her eyes again and smiled.

"Well, letter or no letter, we have to eat. You will be late for school. Come into the kitchen and help bring in the food."

"We must eat quickly, Mother," said Chava. "I'm going to tell Mimi about the letter on my way to school, and Naomi will go and tell Rifka."

"Yes," said Naomi "we have to tell her at once."

"I suppose so," said Sarah, "although you'd think that after over a year another few hours not knowing won't kill anyone."

"Mother!" said Naomi and Chava, shocked.

Sarah laughed: "Did I say you shouldn't go? Me? I said nothing, nothing at all." She led the way into the kitchen, where Dvora and Shoshie were just finishing the last slice of bread and the last egg.

"Dvora! Shoshie! What have you done? You've eaten everyone's breakfast."

"The little fish got hungry," said Dvora. "Swimming made them hungry."

"There are still two eggs left in the water that I was going to use for a salad, and there are some biscuits in the jar. Also take some fruit, Chava, and you, Naomi."

"Aren't you angry?" Dvora wanted to know.

"With a fish?" Sarah laughed. "Who can be angry with a fish? Today, I couldn't be angry with anyone. There is a letter from Isaac, from America."

"Really? Will you read it? Did he say I was the prettiest of all?" Dvora seemed pleased, but not overwhelmed.

"I'll read it to you tonight, after school."

"We're going to the Old Man after school."

"Then at bedtime," said Sarah. "Whenever you want. It doesn't matter. Now, hurry everyone, or we'll grow old and grey in this kitchen."

Later, as Chava, Naomi and Dvora left for school, Sarah shouted at Naomi from the balcony:

"Make very sure that Zehava Gluckmann doesn't hear what you tell Rifka, and invite her to tea tomorrow. And you, Chava, tell Mimi to come. I'm going to bake all day. Goodbye, my darlings, go carefully."

147

Chapter XIV

The next afternoon at three o'clock, the girls and Mimi were sitting in the dining-room waiting for Mrs. Gluckmann to come to tea. Sarah was laying the table with the best china, and Rifka, Chava and Naomi carried the cakes and biscuits in from the kitchen.

"Can't we just nibble a little, Sarah, before she comes?" said Mimi, who was dressed for the occasion in a lilac organdie dress with a frothy skirt.

"You're worse than the girls, Mimi, really you are. Control yourself."

Mimi sighed, then brightened. "You know, Sarah, it's the first time in twenty years you've called me Mimi."

Sarah looked embarrassed. "Yes, I'm sorry." Then she smiled. "But you don't look like a Miriam. A Miriam would never wear a hat like a purple meringue."

Both women started giggling like young girls.

Dvora and Shoshie, who had been waiting on the steps for Mrs. Gluckmann, ran into the room, shouting: "She's coming, she's coming!" and Sarah and Mimi stopped laughing at once.

Mrs. Gluckmann puffed slowly up the steps, and Sarah greeted her at the door.

"Come in, Zehava, come in. Sit down and rest yourself. It's very hot already, isn't it?"

"Like my ovens. Thank you, Sarah my dear." She lowered

herself into a chair, and smiled at Mimi. "Good afternoon, Miss Bernstein."

"Call me Mimi, please, Mrs. Gluckmann."

"Mimi . . ." Mrs. Gluckmann sounded hesitant, as if the word had an unfamiliar taste. "Mimi . . . I thought you were going abroad. To Strasbourg, I heard."

"Well, Mrs. Gluckmann, I'll tell you the truth. I considered it. I had an offer of marriage, you see, but in spite of the fact that the gentleman was handsome, charming and rich, I still feel I can do better."

Mrs. Gluckmann's mouth fell open and Mimi winked at Rifka, Chava and Naomi, as Mrs. Gluckmann turned to Sarah again, bewildered.

"And what do you hear from Isaac, Sarah?" she said.

Sarah began to pour the tea. "Isaac? Oh, we had a lovely letter from him only yesterday. He's doing very well. Milk or lemon? I'll read you a little of what he says after tea. It seems that his employer has a beautiful daughter, but of course, nothing is definite yet. Suger? There. Rifka, please cut the cake."

Mrs. Gluckmann took her tea, and a thick slice of cake.

"I really must send him the photograph of my girls," she said. "I suppose he has seen the one of his sisters."

"Of course," said Rifka, "he was the very first person we gave one to, after Mother, naturally."

"And did he like it?"

"Yes," said Naomi, "although in America, you know, photographs are very common. Everybody has lots and lots."

"How do you know, Naomi?" said Dvora.

"I just do, that's all." Naomi smiled round the table, and began to eat her cake.

149